THE FIRST STEP
A Knight Original

The girl was obviously practising a solo. She spun round in a series of dazzling pirouettes and then seemed to fly across the room, landing with a lightness that suggested an ethereal spirit rather than a flesh and blood girl.

Moth realised that she had been watching an artist . . .

Moth Graham longed to be able to dance as well as that. Now, at last, she had her chance to learn – as a junior pupil at a small but well-known ballet school.

This is the story of Moth's first year there: her ups and downs, successes and failures. It will strike an immediate chord with anyone who, like Moth, has longed to be able to dance.

Jacket illustration by Sarah Simpson, with acknowledgement to the Jeanne du Gay Academy of Dance.

The First Step

Jean Richardson

Illustrated by Priscilla Lamont

KNIGHT BOOKS
Hodder and Stoughton

First published by Knight Books 1979
Second impression 1979

BRITISH LIBRARY C.I.P.
Richardson, Jean
The first step.
I. Title
823'.9'1J PZ7.R/

ISBN 0-340-24030-X

The characters and situations in this book are entirely imaginary and bear no relation to any real person or actual happening.

Printed and bound in Great Britain for
Hodder and Stoughton Paperback, a
division of Hodder and Stoughton Ltd.,
Mill Road, Dunton Green, Sevenoaks,
Kent (Editorial Office: 47 Bedford
Square, London, WC1 3DP) by
Hunt Barnard Printing Ltd.,
Aylesbury, Bucks.

ISBN 0 340 24030 X

Contents

1

No Money

It was failing her audition that started it all. The audition was for a place at White Lodge – the Lower School of the Royal Ballet – and, as Moth soon realised, she was only one of several hundred children who wanted to become dancers.

Moth had been dancing ever since she could remember. Her brother liked to tease her about the photograph of her when she was six, taking part in a Christmas show and wearing what Toby unkindly called her 'soppy swan face'. She hadn't known anything about *Swan Lake* or any other ballet at the time. It was just that her feet wanted to dance, and while other children often found it hard to remember the steps, Moth picked them up at once and easily fitted them to the music.

The Graham family lived in a small country town, so Moth didn't have much chance to go to the ballet. Touring companies sometimes did a week at a big town nearby, but ballet as a form of entertainment, let alone as a way of life, seemed very odd to most people.

Moth wasn't sure why she was so drawn to it. She

certainly didn't get it from her parents, both of whom had their feet very firmly on the ground. She went to dancing classes every week, did well in her grade exams, and had taken part in one or two local festivals, but that was as far as it went.

That is until the day when the guest of honour at a festival noticed Moth and asked her about her dancing. Then she spoke to Moth's teacher, Mrs. Shaw, who in turn spoke to Moth's parents, and as a result Moth auditioned for a place at White Lodge.

The fact that she didn't get one should have settled the matter. But the audition gave Moth ideas. Only when it seemed as though the chance was being taken away from her, did she know that the one thing she really wanted in life was to learn to dance, to dance so well that one day she would get a place in the Royal Ballet Company.

Her parents were amazed at the sudden change in her. Until then she had been a rather quiet, unambitious child with no ideas about the future. Now, overnight, she could talk of nothing but going to a full-time dancing school. They thought it was ridiculous, but they talked it over with Mrs. Shaw, who wasn't at all encouraging.

'It's so hard to say at eleven,' she told them. 'Moth has good proportions and a nice line at the moment, but she could easily grow into quite the wrong shape for a dancer. She could get too tall, or too fat, not have strong enough feet to take the strain, or just simply change her mind. I know you're set on dancing now,' she said, turning to Moth, 'but by the time you're fifteen, you may want to go to university or do something else instead.'

Moth didn't say anything. She knew that it was a waste of time to argue. Grown-ups were always the same. They always saw all the difficulties and drawbacks. They would say things like 'This is a new idea. You didn't want to do this until a few weeks ago.' Whereas Moth felt that deep down she had always wanted to be a dancer, though she hadn't fully realised it until the audition. She knew now that if only they would let her have this one chance, she would work hard, even at the things she hated.

But it was also a question of money. If she had got a place at White Lodge, she would have been given a grant that paid for everything. But most education authorities didn't like giving grants for other schools, at least until you were older, and her county didn't give any at all.

'And it's not just a matter of the fees,' said her mother, when Moth wandered into the kitchen where Mrs. Graham was busy making bread.

'There's no suitable dancing school near here, and it would cost far too much to send you to a boarding school. I'm sorry, darling, but we can't afford it. We've got Toby and Lyn to think of, too.'

'But they don't want to be dancers,' said Moth. 'Toby wants to be a footballer, and that doesn't cost money.'

'Not at the moment,' said her mother, flouring her hands and beginning to knead the sticky ball of dough. 'But one of these days they may get expensive ideas like you, and it wouldn't be fair if we'd spent all our money on you.'

She pulled the dough into an oblong, folded it over and pummelled it again.

'You can go on having lessons with Mrs. Shaw, and then if you're good enough you can have another shot at the Royal school when you're sixteen. If you get in you'll be certain to get a grant.'

Moth couldn't imagine ever being sixteen.

'Mrs. Shaw isn't good enough,' she said furiously. 'Nobody from her school has ever become a real dancer. It's all a game. She doesn't even like ballet all that much. She'd much rather I did tap and modern dancing, like everyone else. I hate you and daddy. You can have the things you want because you're grownup, but I can't wait as long as that. If I'm going to be a proper dancer, I've got to start now, before my bones get set. And you won't let me.'

Moth rushed up stairs, slammed her bedroom door, and burst into tears.

Mrs. Graham went on calmly making bread. She cut up the dough, folded it into the tins, and put them in a warm place until the dough had risen and was ready for baking. Later that afternoon the delicious smell of fresh bread crept through the house.

Moth heard Toby begging for a crust off the new warm loaf. Usually they fought over it, but today she didn't feel hungry. She stood in front of the mirror and began to practise her pliés. Her feet were in the second position, so that they formed a straight line, but she was still too young for her hips and whole leg to turn out. She looked at herself mournfully. Supposing Mrs. Shaw wasn't strict enough. By the time she was sixteen it would be too late to correct really bad habits.

She sat down on her bed and tried to think of a way out. She could run away. But where to? She could give

up eating so that she got thinner and thinner, and then they'd be sorry. But she didn't really feel she could keep it up, especially when she could smell new bread. She had no money and no way of making any. 'It's so unfair,' she thought. 'I bet if Toby suddenly wanted to be a doctor, they'd do everything they could to help him. Why is dancing so different?'

*

'But it's not as though we'd be investing in a worthwhile career,' said Mr. Graham, as he and his wife talked it over a few days later. 'I want Moth to be happy, and I hate to see her going round like a wet week, but this dancing lark is so uncertain. I've been making some more enquiries, and there's no safe job at the end of all this training. You have to be brilliant and lucky to get into this Royal Ballet, and even then if you have an accident you can be off work for weeks and perhaps never dance again. It sounds like a recipe for heartache to me.'

And Mr. Graham sank deeper into his armchair and sucked his pipe for comfort, as he always did when he brought a problem home from the office.

'Well, security isn't everything,' said Mrs. Graham. She was more romantic than her husband, and thought she knew how Moth felt.

'She'll make herself ill if she goes on like this. She's been so moody lately, and she's lost all interest in school. If only it didn't cost so much, I'd be for giving her a chance. She's more likely to do well at other subjects if she's happy, and if she passes her O levels there'll be plenty of time to make plans for the future once she's over this dancing craze. At least it's teaching her to move gracefully. We should be glad she doesn't want to be a pop star.'

'That's all very well,' said Mr. Graham, looking crossly at his pipe, 'but who's going to pay for all this? Moth would have to go away to school, and you know we can't afford that.'

He lent forward, switched on the T.V., and relaxed as the titles of one of his favourite programmes slid onto the screen. As far as he was concerned, he felt that the matter was settled.

But Mrs. Graham was worried by Moth's sullen silence. She didn't discuss it with her husband any more, but she tried to think of some way of finding the money. She had been trained as a teacher, and had always meant to go back to teaching once the children were old enough to manage without her. Lyn was at school now, but Mrs. Graham liked them to have someone to come home to. She didn't want them to become latch-key children. Besides, even if she did do some part-time teaching, it wouldn't bring in enough money to send Moth to boarding school.

However, as some extra money would certainly be useful, she decided to ask the local authority if they needed any teachers. Her letter coincided with urgent plans for new day-release courses, and to her surprise and delight Mrs. Graham found herself in demand. Mr. Graham huffed and puffed a bit about working wives and mothers, but he wasn't a selfish man at heart and he had to admit that it was too good a chance to miss.

All the excitement inspired second thoughts about Moth's future and led to Mrs. Graham making still further enquiries. The school she liked the sound of best was small and in London, and it didn't take boarders, but just when it seemed that the problem of how and where Moth would live couldn't be solved, Fate took a hand.

The answer came from a most unexpected source that everyone had forgotten, and it involved someone that Moth hardly knew.

2

Doubts

'You must remember,' said Mr. Graham, as the car sped along the motorway towards London, 'that Great-Aunt Marion is an elderly lady. Life was very different when she was your age, and although I'm sure she'll do her best, you'll have to meet her halfway.'

Moth was silent. She was still dazed by the speed with which her whole life had suddenly been turned upside down. She could still hardly believe that she was leaving home and going to live with a remote great-aunt in a strange city in order to go to a new kind of school. It was enough to silence anyone, especially someone who had never been away from home before, except to spend a few days with her best friend. Now she didn't even have a best friend any more.

'Penny for your thoughts,' said her father, as the countryside rushed past at the same breathless speed as Moth's new life.

Moth sighed. How could she begin to explain that after wanting something so badly, getting it wasn't somehow the thrill she had thought it would be. There were so many plans to be made and so much responsibility. And then supposing she wasn't any good at dancing? Supposing that when she tried, her body became earthbound and her feet wouldn't obey her? Wouldn't they all think – her parents, who were spending so much money on her, Great-Aunt Marion, whose offer of a home during term time had made the dream come true, Mrs. Shaw, the new school – that she had let them down?

Her father thought he understood.

'You can always come back if you don't like it, you know. But now we've got this far, I think you should give it a fair try. We don't want you to grow up into one of those people who go round feeling they've never had a chance. If you don't like dancing after all, or if it doesn't like you, you'll have got it out of your system, and then we can find something you like better. So cheer up, and stop looking as though it's the end of the world. We're nearly there, and I need somebody wide awake to do a bit of map reading and tell me where to go.'

Great-Aunt Marion lived at the top of a large old house. It had been built in the days when houses didn't have to be squeezed into tiny spaces, and when families had lots of children and so needed lots of rooms and large gardens. Great-Aunt Marion had been born in the house and had lived there all her life. Her four brothers had left home to get married or work in distant parts of the world like Australia, and when her sister died and she found herself alone, she had sensibly converted the house into flats.

Although it meant climbing up two flights of stairs,

she had kept the top flat for herself. She liked living at the top because she could look down over the garden and into the ones on either side, and every spring she had a bird's eye-view of apple and cherry trees laden with blossom.

Although David Graham had been her favourite nephew when he was a small boy, she hadn't seen much of him since he had taken a job in the Midlands, and she hadn't seen Moth for several years. So neither of them knew quite what to expect.

When she opened the door, Marion Graham saw a thin, rather anxious-looking child with a pale face, tawny eyes, and long straight hair. Moth saw a tall, elegantly dressed woman. She had a very straight back, a forbidding expression, and white hair that was swept back from her face and pinned up in a very neat French pleat. Moth's heart sank. She didn't look at all like the kind of dear old lady who would make a fuss of her and not ask awkward questions. Her eyes were very alert, and she had an air of authority, as though she was used to giving orders and making sure that they were obeyed.

As they had driven a long way and Mr. Graham had to start back almost at once, Great-Aunt Marion had prepared a high tea. But Moth didn't feel hungry. She looked with dismay at the lace tablecloth and the delicate flowered china and thought wistfully of the stout mugs they used at home. There they had tea round the kitchen table and Toby fought her for the bun with the most currants or the right to scrape out the jam jar. Great-Aunt Marion didn't look as though she would allow fights at her table, and everything was so dainty and fragile that Moth felt she might easily break a cup or drop jam on the spotless cloth.

'At least the grub's good,' said her father with a wink, as he helped himself to another homemade scone. 'You'll probably get so used to all this good living that we'll seem a very uncouth lot when you come home.'

'I wish I was home now,' said Moth passionately, and the tears that she had been holding back all the journey threatened to spill over.

Just then Great-Aunt Marion came back from the kitchen with a mountain of hot sausage rolls, so Moth didn't have a chance to explain why she felt so miserable.

After tea they went to see Moth's room. It was up

steep narrow stairs and tucked right under the roof. In parts the ceiling sloped down to the floor, and unlike the little box of a room that Moth shared with Lyn, there was so much space that she would be able to practise here. Everything looked old and well worn. There was a patchwork quilt on the bed, a collection of odd cupboards, and a small chest of drawers with an old-fashioned swing mirror on it. But the most striking piece of furniture in the room – to which Moth lost her heart at once – was a curious little desk. It was open to show a flap lined with faded green leather and two rows of intriguing little drawers, and it was obviously very old because it had two ornate gilt candlesticks which showed that it had been made in the days before people had gas or electric lighting.

Moth longed to explore the desk to see if it had any secret drawers, but she didn't like to do this in front of her great-aunt. Yet the sight of the desk cheered her up and somehow made the moment when she had to say goodbye to her father a little easier.

'Keep your pecker up,' he said, as he opened the car door. 'You'll find your great-aunt's quite human underneath that starchy exterior, and I expect you'll soon be so busy that you won't have time to miss us.'

'I will, I will,' said Moth, throwing her arms round his neck and breathing in the comforting smell of his tobacco. 'I wish I'd never wanted to dance. I wish I was still having lessons with Mrs. Shaw and going to school with Jenny.'

Her father rumpled the top of her hair. The last few weeks had been hard for him, too. His wife had insisted on taking a job – a thing he didn't really like – and all because his daughter was mad about dancing. Now she seemed to have changed her mind. What was a man to do?

He didn't understand why Moth was so unsure of herself, so he decided that the trouble must be that she was beginning to feel homesick.

'It's a big break, I know, but everyone has to leave home and find themselves sooner or later. I never went away to school myself, but I knew lots of boys who did, and in the past children had to do all sorts of nasty things by themselves.' Mr. Graham racked his brains for an example. He wished that his wife was with him. 'Remember that little boy in *The Water Babies* who had to climb chimneys? Eleven isn't too soon to be striking out on your own if you've found something you really want to do. Think of it as a great adventure, with you as the heroine who has to battle away all by herself. At the worst you've only got to last out until Christmas, then you can tell us all about your ordeal and change your mind if you want to. And talking of Christmas reminds me. Here's a little good-luck present to open when I've gone.'

Moth took the small packet, gave her father a last hug and kiss, and watched him ease the car away from the kerb and drive off into the evening sunlight. She loved him as much as ever, but she realised that she had taken the first step into a world that she wouldn't be able to share with him. She walked up the path and sat down on one of the chipped stone steps leading up to the front door. Then she undid the packet.

Inside was a box padded with cotton wool. It protected the little silver figure of a dancer attached to a silver chain. There was a card that read: 'To wish our dancer luck, with lots of love from Mummy and Daddy.'

Moth undid the clasp, put the chain round her neck and tucked it inside her shirt. Then she went round to the side door that led up to the top flat, went in and shut the door behind her. She could feel the cold shape of the dancer against her skin as she ran up the stairs to face her great-aunt and the future.

3

A New World

The days before term started firmly marked off Moth's old life from her new one. A few things came with her, such as a photograph of the family sitting on the beach and looking just as she liked to think of them, and her collection of Degas postcards.

She had been collecting these for several years, and it had become something of a family tradition to send her ballet cards, often of paintings by Degas, at Christmas and birthdays. Although the dancers he drew and painted were all dead now, because he worked about a hundred years ago, Moth felt that they were very real to her and lived in a world she longed to enter. Degas had caught them off stage and on, tying their shoes, rehearsing in a studio, taking a bow, and had understood and captured the hardship and attraction of a dancer's life.

Moth would like to have stuck the cards up in her bedroom – there were acres of empty walls – but she felt too shy to ask her great-aunt if she would mind. It was hard to work out quite simple things like this, because her great-aunt's lifestyle was so different from that of Moth's parents.

For one thing, it was so quiet and orderly. There was no shouting, no rushing around, no family squabbles, and no television. She firmly disapproved of television and told Moth so quite sharply. Her days had a regular pattern: she liked to read the morning paper with her breakfast; then she would go shopping and change her library books; in the afternoon she went for a walk or had a friend to tea; and after supper she would either read or play Patience.

Moth knew that she wanted her to be happy, but it wasn't easy to fit into such a strict routine. She had to make her own bed, tidy her room, help with the washing up, and do her homework. But what then? Great-Aunt Marion's answer seemed to be: reading.

Even her food was different. Great-Aunt Marion didn't eat crisps, fish fingers, hamburgers, chips, potatoes in their jackets, or ice cream. She took a great deal of trouble preparing proper dishes and odd vegetables; in the first week Moth discovered that she liked avocados, wasn't sure about artichoke soup, and hated aubergines.

One useful thing her great-aunt did know was where to buy Moth three pairs of soft ballet shoes and the dark blue leotard which was the only uniform the school insisted on. They went to a funny little shop that had been making ballet shoes for years; the walls were lined with photographs of their famous customers, and Moth hoped they would want one of her some day. Then, to her surprise, her great-aunt took her round the corner to a bookshop that seemed to have every book on ballet that had ever been written. The shelves spilt over onto a counter stacked with magazines and trays of photographs.

'I thought you might like one or two for your room, to inspire you,' she said, as though she could read Moth's thoughts.

There were hundreds of photographs to sort through, but Moth finally chose one of Anthony Dowell and his most famous partner, Antoinette Sibley, doing a fish dive, which looked exciting and difficult, and a poster of Natalia Makarova, the beautiful Russian dancer who ran away from the Kirov Ballet to dance in the West. She was poised on tiptoe with one leg and her arms stretching away into the distance.

'One day I shall see her dance,' Moth promised herself, 'but just looking at her arabesque makes me feel that's how I'd like to be.'

Apart from making sure that she had everything on the school list, Moth also found out exactly where the school was. She dreaded having to turn up in the custody of her great-aunt, and as it was only a short walk from the flat, she begged to be allowed to go on her own.

'Not on the first day and certainly not across that main road,' said her great-aunt firmly. 'Everyone'll have a parent or adult with them, and your parents would expect me to take their place.'

Moth thought wistfully of her mother, who would drop her outside and drive off with an unembarrassing wave. Being escorted by a white-haired elderly lady, however well-meaning, was very different.

Unlike Moth's previous schools this one had once been a private house, though a very grand one. It had belonged to a fashionable Victorian artist, who had given wild parties in the elegant drawing-room, had lots of friends to stay in the maze of bedrooms, swung in a hammock under the apple trees in the untidy garden, and painted huge pictures of beautiful women in a barn-like studio at the bottom of the garden.

The studio had now been turned into a theatre, the drawing-room still had a grand piano but was now lined with mirrors and practice barres, the library was still a library, the study now belonged to Miss Lambert, the principal, and all the bedrooms had been turned into classrooms. Most of the garden had disappeared under the playground, but a few flowering trees still lingered on and there was grass thick with clover beyond the studio. The most obvious change was the tremendous noise and bustle.

The din reached right out onto the pavement. To her relief Moth saw that there was an odd assortment of adults; she was glad that at least her great-aunt wasn't holding onto her, unlike one very determined-looking mother who was grasping a reluctant small boy. Moth was surprised to see that he wasn't as tall as she was, though she guessed that they would be in the same class. She noticed several men festooned with cameras and flash guns waiting in the road, but before she could ask her great-aunt who they were expecting, a sleek car drew up and they snapped into action. A chauffeur got out and ran round to open the other door, but to Moth's disappointment instead of a famous dancer a girl of about her own age got out. She had a fringe and hair tied in bunches of ringlets, and she was obviously used to photographers. She smiled briefly and then walked up the path, followed by the chauffeur who was carrying a dainty blue leather case. Moth said a hurried goodbye and tried to pretend that she wasn't afraid.

The noise inside was deafening. Girls giggled, chattered and squealed as they pushed their way to a large notice-board covered with lists. They jostled

satchels, music cases and plastic carriers stuffed with books and clothes. Some of them had already changed into practice dress and were swathed in heavy sweaters, cardigans, and thick woolly leg-warmers. Somewhere in the background a piano was already pounding out the routine of a class.

Suddenly a girl appeared at the top of the stairs and started ringing an old-fashioned handbell. The chattering rose to a crescendo and then faded away down the corridors. Soon the hall was empty apart from a handful of lost looking girls, the unwilling small boy and a lanky boy with fizzing curly hair. Like Moth, they were newcomers.

Afterwards Moth realised that she had hardly said a word all day. There was so much to take in, so many things to remember. There were lockers, classrooms and desks to sort out. There were instructions on how to get ready for a class, where to change, how to put your hair up, how to darn your shoes and sew the ribbons on. There was the timetable to copy down, a timetable that was disappointingly full of English, French, maths, and geography, and only allowed an hour or so a day for dancing, with extra classes on Saturdays.

There were six other girls and two boys in Moth's form. One of them was the girl with ringlets, who told them that her name was Selsey James and, when no one seemed impressed, that she was a film star and someone very special.

'I've just flown over for a term,' she said, 'to get some background for my next picture in which I'm playing a brilliant child ballerina. My director knows the head of this school and she just begged him to let me come here. I expect she could do with some free publicity.'

Nobody said anything. Moth was relieved to see that the rest of the class looked more ordinary and that like herself they were too shy to talk about themselves. She found herself sitting in between a tall thin girl called Jane and a round plump one called Ruth, who had a happy smile but seemed an unlikely shape for a future ballerina. The two boys, Tom of the forceful mother and the curly-haired Drew, had desks in the row behind them.

By the afternoon Moth felt that she couldn't take in any more new ideas and people, but her most disturbing experience was still to come. The new girls had been told that they were expected to make their own skirts for character dancing and that Mrs. George, who looked after the wardrobe, would tell them what material to buy. The wardrobe was at the top of the house, in what had once been the attics, but Moth couldn't find any stairs leading up to it. She was wandering along the top corridor, peering into corners in the hope of finding the elusive staircase, when she heard music coming from one of the rooms. The door was half open, so she tiptoed up and looked inside.

The walls were lined with mirrors as in all the practice rooms, and at first it looked as though there were several figures dancing and not just one. The music came from a tape-recorder and the girl in the room was concentrating all her attention on it. She was small and doll-like, and her arms and legs looked so fragile that Moth felt they could easily snap. Her black hair was cut into a straight fringe above enormous dark eyes, and although her face was not pretty and seemed too grownup for the rest of her, it was not a face that was easy to forget. But it was not her face that silenced Moth as she stood in the doorway.

The girl was obviously practising a solo. She spun round in a series of dazzling pirouettes and then seemed to fly across the room, landing with a lightness that suggested an ethereal spirit rather than a flesh and blood girl. Her arms had an instinctive grace and Moth, who was always being told to relax her fingers, noticed that her hands made a beautiful shape. Her final attitude had such control that she seemed to freeze into stillness.

Until she saw Moth.

'What do you want?' she said angrily. 'How dare you come snooping round here. This room is private and no one is allowed in, so get out.'

She stormed towards the door, eyes blazing. She was not much taller than Moth although she was obviously older, but her anger was the more terrifying because it was so unexpected. She was not just cross because she had been disturbed while practising. Moth realised that she had been watching an artist, and that talent of this order wasn't kind or considerate. It was unreasonable, determined, and ruthless, and it was dangerous to get in its way.

She fled down to the cloakroom and seized her things. She wanted to run home to the things and people she understood; but then she remembered. Home was hundreds of miles away and waiting outside was not her mother, longing to hear all about her first day, but the distant figure of Great-Aunt Marion.

4

Caught Out

By the end of a fortnight Moth had convinced her great-aunt that she knew the way to school, that she would look both ways first and not dash across the main road, that she wouldn't speak to strangers and wouldn't accept lifts. She realised that her great-aunt meant well when she fussed, but she made Moth feel rather like Timmy Willie, the timid little country mouse in the Beatrix Potter story, who came to London by accident when he fell asleep in a pea pod and was no match for the sharp Johnny Town-Mouse who rescued him. Although she found London bewildering, Moth was determined not to be a country mouse.

She was gradually getting used to the new ways of the school, and although she hadn't made a best friend yet, she and Ruth often chose each other as partners.

Drama was the best lesson for getting to know the others. In one of the first lessons everyone had been asked why they wanted to dance and what kind of dancing they had done so far. The idea was to get them talking naturally in front of the class, but Selsey, who expected to be the star of any drama around, was peeved to find that even here she couldn't get away from dancing and come out on top. Although she looked very balletic in her leotard and would stand round as though she was posing for a photograph, she didn't know much more than the five positions and was soon in trouble.

'I don't care if you never dance a step afterwards,' said Miss Pearson, as she tried yet again to turn Selsey's knees out. 'While you're in my class you'll at least try to do the exercises properly.'

Selsey made a face behind Miss Pearson's back, but no one laughed because class was a serious business. They all knew that they would have to accept the daily routine of class for the rest of their dancing lives, and that even the greatest dancers needed the discipline of a class to keep their bodies supple and correct any faults.

Moth was dismayed to find that her shoulders and arms were often too stiff, and Miss Pearson was always finding fault with her, or so it seemed. She was no longer the star pupil, and she felt rather like Alice when the Red Queen told her, 'It takes all the running *you* can do, to stay in the same place. If you want to get somewhere else, you must run at least twice as fast as that!' She could see in the mirror that Ruth, for all her plumpness, had far more control, and she despaired of ever looking as elegant as Jane.

Selsey never missed a chance to show that she didn't think much of dancing.

'I wouldn't want to be a dancer,' she said, when it was her turn to tell the class about her career. 'Dancers don't earn big money like actresses, and they aren't famous in the same way. When I go shopping lots of people recognise me because they've seen my films, but who cares about dancers? And then dancers give up when they're still quite young, but I'm going to go on and on acting until I'm very old. There are lots of famous old actresses, but who's ever heard of an old dancer?'

'What about Margot Fonteyn?' asked Tom. He was already making a name for himself because he could somersault like an acrobat and jump higher than anyone else. 'She started dancing years ago, and she still appears in special performances.'

'I've seen her,' said Jane, 'and she was fabulous.'

Jane's parents had lots of money and a box at Covent Garden. They were always taking Jane to the ballet, and the next day she could talk about nothing else and made all the others boast about the ballets they'd seen.

This kind of showing off made Moth uncomfortable. She had only seen a few ballets and these had not been danced by the top stars. She had never been to Covent Garden and wasn't even sure where it was, but if she was to keep up with the others, she would obviously have to go there as soon as possible.

She found out that the current programme was pinned up on the notice-board in the hall, and saw that ballets were not put on every night but spaced out between the operas. The leading male dancer of the company was still Anthony Dowell, though he wasn't dancing very often and only once in *La Fille mal gardée*, the one ballet that Moth had to see.

They were learning about famous choreographers in the ballet history class, and this term Mrs. Fraser had decided to concentrate on Sir Frederick Ashton, whose marvellous ballets had helped to transform a group of aspiring dancers into a great national company. Mrs. Fraser told them the story of *La Fille mal gardée* and played a tape of the catchy clog dance tune, and it turned out that nearly everyone had seen it because it was such a popular happy ballet that the Royal Ballet companies were always dancing in it.

'I've seen Michael Coleman, David Wall, and Anthony Dowell as Colas,' said Jane, and at once everyone was joining in with shouts of who they'd seen and who they thought danced best.

'How about you, Moth,' said Mrs. Fraser, 'have you seen it?'

Before she could think of the consequences, Moth heard herself saying, 'Oh yes. I saw Anthony Dowell and he was magic. It's my favourite ballet.'

'Good,' said Mrs. Fraser. 'Well, in that case, perhaps you'd like to do it as your special project. You can each choose an Ashton ballet, find out all you can about it, and then give a little talk about what you've discovered.'

She went on to tell them what books to look in to find out the story, who wrote the music and designed the scenery and costumes, and who were the first dancers to create the parts, but Moth didn't hear a word she said. How could she tell the others about a ballet they had all seen but she hadn't? How could she own up to such a silly white lie? It was too late to choose another ballet, one she could research just from books. There was only one way out: somehow she had to go to the one performance at which Dowell was dancing.

She was so quiet and withdrawn that evening and ate so little that her great-aunt was concerned.

'I hope you're not sickening for something,' she said, putting her hand on Moth's forehead, which was burning with thought. 'Perhaps you'd better go to bed early with an aspirin and a glass of hot milk.'

Moth was so preoccupied that she forgot to say that she hated hot milk. She was thinking of how to get to the vital performance, and the only way seemed to be to ask her great-aunt to come with her. Perhaps if Moth offered to pay for the tickets she would be willing, and it might help to say that the school had said that she had to go.

'I want to go to Covent Garden next month,' she said nervously, 'I have to do a project on one of the ballets and I need to see it. Daddy gave me some money for emergencies and extra expenses, and I'm sure he'd call this a good cause. It's at 7.30 on a Friday, so I could sleep late the next day; and I'd like you to come as my guest.'

Her great-aunt smiled. 'What a lovely idea. I can't remember the last time I went to the ballet. I'll ring up first thing tomorrow, and it must certainly be my treat.'

Moth ought to have slept well now that the problem seemed to be solved, but she had an anxious dream in which she was supposed to be going to the theatre but it kept disappearing. It was always just round the corner or at the top of the next street, but whenever she got there it had vanished.

At breakfast she reminded her great-aunt about the tickets, and as soon as she got home she rushed up the stairs and gasped, 'Are we going?'

'I'm afraid not,' said her great-aunt. 'You seem to have picked a very popular night and all the tickets have been sold. I'm sorry you're so disappointed,' she added, for Moth was looking horror-struck, 'but we'll try and book for the next programme. I expect there's something else you'd like to see.'

There wasn't. Moth went up to her room and sat down on the bed. She couldn't bear to look up at the photograph of Dowell on the wall. Even if she read every book about Ashton and his ballets, she was sure that the others would guess that she hadn't actually seen one, that she'd told a lie. Not surprisingly she had been worse than ever at class today. She hadn't even put her hair up properly, and it had come tumbling down halfway through. Could it be that she wasn't destined to be a dancer after all? That she would never be able to compete with girls like the fiery temperamental Marina – whom she'd since discovered was the school's star pupil – or the self-assured Jane? Perhaps ballet was a superior world to which you either belonged – or you didn't.

5

Floral Street

By now Moth knew her way round the school and had no trouble finding the sewing room, where she was to make her character skirt with the expert help of Mrs. George. She began the class with a little pep talk about how important it was for dancers to be able to sew.

'And it's not just a question of sewing ribbons on your shoes and darning the toes to stop them wearing out so fast. You don't know what you may have to do once you join a company, and you won't be much use to them if you can't take your turn at the sewing machine.'

'I bet you don't have to do that at Covent Garden,' said Jane, who was finding it hard enough to fold her skirt material the right way. 'My mother says they have a proper wardrobe staff who look after all the costumes and mend and iron them.'

'And what makes you think you'll be dancing at Covent Garden?' said Mrs. George, showing Moth how to pin on the pattern. 'Only a very few dancers ever get into the Royal Ballet. Most of you, if you're lucky, will probably end up in small companies struggling to make both ends meet, and you'll have to do worse things than a little sewing. But before you get that far, and when you've made your skirts, I should like some help with the Christmas show. We're very proud of the fact that we never hire any costumes here. Everything's made by hand, and we're famous for our beautiful displays.'

There were plenty of photographs on the walls to confirm this, and as Moth looked up at the rows of past angels, kings and shepherds, she saw miles of sewing ahead.

She had been to the notice-board several times to have another look at the Covent Garden programme. She kept hoping that they might have decided to cancel one of the operas and put on another performance of *La Fille* – by special request – but the management didn't seem to have thought of this. Then her eye was caught by the words 'Booking on the day,' and she read:

> 65 Rear Amphitheatre seats are available from 10am on the day of performance (personal booking only). A limit of 1 per applicant will be made if demand is high.

This was obviously the answer. Somehow she had got to be there at ten o'clock to get one of those tickets. The only problem was how?

Moth was not quite sure why she didn't tell her great-aunt and ask her advice. Perhaps it was because she doubted whether an elderly lady, however active, would be willing to get up early on a cold November morning to stand in a queue. Perhaps it was because she knew that if her great-aunt said no, it would be an act of deliberate defiance to go against her wishes. And Moth didn't want to be disobedient. But even if she was able to get a ticket, how could she go without telling her great-aunt, who would surely never let her go out late at night by herself?

Moth thought about the problem so much that several lessons passed her by, but it was impossible to daydream in class when they were doing exercises to the irresistible beat of Russell Watson. He had unruly red hair and had to earn his living as an accompanist while writing a symphony at home in the evenings. He was inclined to be downcast when it wasn't going very well, but when he was in a good mood he could make up just the right tune for any set of steps.

Eventually Moth worked out a plan: to get to Covent Garden she would tell her great-aunt that she had to go to school early for an extra lesson, and then she would explain her late arrival at school by saying that she had not felt well. As a truthful person she was worried about having to tell lies – and she couldn't convince herself that they weren't lies – but she decided that they were part of the sacrifice she must make if she wanted to be a great dancer. She did want to be honest, but it wasn't her fault that all the tickets had gone and Fate hadn't come up with any other way.

She was also worried about how to get to Covent Garden. She was scared of the vastness of London with its warren of back streets behind the famous names such as Oxford Street and the Strand. There was an underground station called Covent Garden, but was it really near the opera house or some kind of joke like Piccadilly Circus, that all Londoners knew wasn't the kind of circus that had acrobats and elephants?

That morning she woke up far too early. It was still dark, but the street lamp outside dappled the sloping ceiling. She could just see Anthony Dowell catching Sibley across his knee as she dived into his arms. Moth thought of the deceptions that lay ahead and the perils of the unknown city. At home she knew all the streets and shops, and as she grew up they seemed to have become smaller and closer together. But she couldn't piece London together at all, and she thought that if she had been a bird at that moment, she would not have known which way to fly to make sure of landing on Covent Garden.

But it wasn't so difficult. Her great-aunt didn't ask

any awkward last-minute questions, and Moth raced to the station, hardly aware of a grey November chill that drove people gladly into the crowded warmth of the Underground. The trains were so packed that at first she was afraid to squeeze in, and she remembered her father reading that in Japan they had special people whose job it was to cram as many people as possible into the carriages. But even they surely wouldn't have found room for any more. Jammed up against a fat woman with an equally fat brief case, a spiked umbrella and something odd with wheels, Moth could hardly turn her head to catch sight of the station names. Baker Street . . . Oxford Circus . . . Piccadilly. She shot out onto the platform and was swept along passageways and down another escalator to the Piccadilly line. At Covent Garden station she wasn't tempted to run up the grimy spiral staircase but waited impatiently for a creaking lift that seemed to belong in a museum.

It was now nearly nine o'clock, but where was the opera house? A newspaper-seller sensed her desperation and said, 'Lost something, miss?'

'I'm looking for Covent Garden,' said Moth.

'Well, you've come to the right place, ain't you,' he said with a laugh, 'unless you want the old market. That's gorn to the other side of London.'

'No, I want the opera house, where they do ballets.'

'Dancer are you?' said the man. 'Well, just you dance round the corner, cross the road and go along Floral Street. You can't miss it.'

And she didn't, though she was surprised that it was such an ordinary little street. Ordinary, that is, on one side. On the other, a handsome cream building soared up.

It was the side of the opera house, and beyond the magic words 'Amphitheatre' and 'Stage Door' were vast doors tall enough to admit the scenery for even the loftiest opera or ballet. Opposite was a kind of shop with the sign 'Box Office', and outside was an alarmingly long queue. It stretched almost to the corner of Floral Street, and by the time Moth had reached the end she had almost given up hope.

The last person in the queue was a young man in an overcoat so large that it seemed to be wearing him rather than the other way about. The collar was turned up to protect his ears and the back of his neck, but chunks of dark wavy hair were just visible above it. He wore glasses, and was so intent on reading a book that he didn't notice Moth.

'Please,' she said rather timidly, 'is this the queue for tonight?'

'I hope so,' he said. 'I wouldn't want to stand round in this cold if it wasn't.'

'It looks a very long queue. Do you think we'll get tickets?'

'Sure to,' he said confidently, 'they're always limited to one each when there's a crowd, and if you count you'll see that there aren't sixty-five people yet.'

Moth checked. It was difficult to count the huddle of anoraks and duffle coats tucked into doorways or perched on stools. The stinging cold bit into hands and feet and some people were sheltering in cars and cafés, taking turns to relieve their partner or bring them a hot mug of coffee. It seemed worth taking a chance.

By the time they finally reached the box office, Moth had learned quite a lot about the queue system and about the young man, whose name was Robert. He told her that as he couldn't afford any other seats he always came on the day – and he had always been lucky. He said he liked ballet and he loved opera, and he'd seen all the most famous dancers and singers.

'I've met some extraordinary people doing this,' he said, unaware that Moth had decided that he was rather an extraordinary person, 'but it's easier at this time of year, when most of the tourist hordes have gone home. In summer it's like the United Nations.'

Moth held her breath when it was her turn at the window. There was no need to speak. The man pushed the ticket across to her as though he were a machine. For him it was a daily chore, but for Moth it was victory.

6

The Back Row

Getting away from her great-aunt was the next problem. After supper and the washing up Moth usually did her homework while her great-aunt read or listened to the radio. Moth liked to work in her room, so that she could sit at the green leather desk with the gilt candlesticks. She longed to have tall candles flickering in them, but her great-aunt was terrified of fire and had absolutely forbidden it. Moth had found a bunch of old seals in one of the drawers, and she imagined one of the desk's previous owners melting his wax at the candles to seal his letters. One of the seals said 'Forget me not' underneath a little flower, and she wondered whose letters had been sealed with this.

The day before, sitting there holding the seal as though it were a lucky charm, she had decided that the best plan was to leave a note for her great-aunt. She had thought of saying that someone at school had given her a ticket, but this would only lead to embarrassing questions about who she was going with and, more important still, who would see her home. It seemed best to leave a simple message:

'Had to go to Covent Garden. Please don't worry. I shall come straight home.'

She would have to miss supper to get there in time, and she realised that her great-aunt would find out that she had gone when she called up to Moth to come and lay the table. She might well think of ringing up the school, or Moth's parents, or even the police, so the best place to leave the note seemed to be under the dial of the telephone. That way her great-aunt wouldn't be able to call anyone without first seeing the note.

Her great-aunt was in the kitchen when Moth tiptoed down the stairs. There was a delicious smell coming from the oven and the appetising warmth made the chill blackness outside seem even more daunting. The street-lights cast patches of light but in between were the strange shadows of walls, bushes, hedges, trees. There was no one about, and as Moth ran along her feet echoed and she was boxed in by a rim of parked cars and the blank darkness of a disused tennis court. It was beginning to rain, and even the orange lighting of the main road looked cold.

But Floral Street was bright and crowded: there were people trying to sell tickets at the last moment, waiting for friends, fumbling in bags and wallets for tickets and change for programmes, stampeding up the stone stairs with an energy that warmed their hands and feet. Up and up. Moth felt they would never get there as each bend in the staircase disappeared on round. And then suddenly there were bars and foyers, attendants with programmes, and the theatre itself, falling down in a blaze of lights past tiers of gilded boxes to an enormous stage curtained in red velvet. Far below she could see the stands of the orchestra with tiny figures tuning up, and as she made her way to P 15 in the last row of all, Moth felt that she might easily lose her balance and go hurtling down into the distant stalls.

Robert was still engrossed in a book. He had shed his overcoat but was now dwarfed by an enormous pair of binoculars that looked more suitable for sighting enemy submarines.

'I'll let you have a look,' he said generously, 'so that you can actually see Dowell's face. You get a marvellous view from up here, and all the best people, the ones who really love ballet and don't just come because their firm pays for the tickets or because it's the O.K. thing to do, sit up here.'

Moth wondered where Jane and her parents usually sat. Were they the best sort of people, in the sense that Robert meant?

Robert told her that she must have a programme as a souvenir. They cost nearly as much as a book, but after a few minutes of looking longingly at Robert's, Moth knew that she had to have one. She needed to know all about this ballet, starting with the story.

It is a simple one of two young lovers who are determined to marry although the girl's mother doesn't approve of the match. She wants her daughter to marry a ridiculous rich young man who cares more for his beautiful red umbrella than for any girl. Moth loved the dance in which the lovers teased each other with long ribbons, spinning round until they were bound together and then weaving the ribbons into a giant cat's cradle. The ballerina was full of mischief and Dowell looked very handsome leaping joyously around and lifting his partner as though she weighed no more than thistledown.

The laughter and high spirits spread to the audience. They loved the little Shetland pony that trotted on drawing a cart to take Lise and her mother to the hayfield, and they cheered the widow's famous clog dance, done in true pantomime style by a male character dancer. The tune was so irresistible that Moth longed to join in, and she was disappointed that there wasn't an encore.

In the interval Robert took her on a grand tour, telling her about all the dancers he'd seen and pointing out a faded costume in a glass case which had once been worn by the great dancer Nijinsky. She liked Robert because he took it for granted that she cared as much about ballet as he did and he talked to her as though they were the same age.

The second act went all too quickly and they stayed until the very last curtain. Moth had never imagined so many curtain calls: the widow, the silly young man and his father, Lise and Colas together, and then an even greater roar for all of them on their own. Someone in a box was throwing flowers on the stage, and Dowell picked one up and presented it to Lise. She had already carried off an armful of bouquets.

Then came a race down the stairs and they burst out into a wet night full of jostling umbrellas and shiny limousines swallowing up couples in evening dress. Moth felt lost.

'Which way do you go?' said Robert, who had retrieved his vast overcoat and was getting ready to dash through the rain. 'Bus or tube?'

'Tube, please,' said Moth, and he took her hand and ran. Although the station was only round the corner, Moth was dampened by more than rain, as Robert noticed.

'Far to go?' he said, and as though sensing her fear, 'Perhaps I'm going your way.'

The Underground was a different place at night. Voices bounced back from empty passages. The din of laughter sounded menacing. A noisy gang just ahead of them grabbed each other with a playfulness that bordered on violence.

'I've only just come to live in London,' said Moth in a rush, 'so I'm not very good at stations and where to change. My great-aunt didn't know where I was going, or she wouldn't have let me travel by myself.'

Robert didn't ask any more questions but he seemed to understand the situation. 'I think I'd better see you all the way home,' he said firmly. 'It's late and a rotten night, and we don't want a future Fonteyn gobbled up by the wolves of St. John's Wood.'

Moth giggled. 'It's not a real wood. It's all houses, though some of them do have big trees in their gardens.'

'Ah, but it used to be a wood once upon a time,' said Robert knowledgeably, 'and you never know. The odd wolf may have survived somehow, and they're very partial to little girls. Think what happened to Red Riding Hood.'

The idea took Moth's mind off the awful moment when she would have to face her great-aunt, and they played a game about a wolf whose name, according to Robert, was Osbert and who spent his time lurking round gardens trying to find his way back to the wood and puzzled by how the world had changed.

They each embroidered the story until it became more and more ridiculous, and as they came up the escalator at St. John's Wood, Moth was quite looking forward to looking out for Osbert on the way home. But as they reached the ticket barrier a figure stepped forward to meet them.

It was Great-Aunt Marion, and she looked very angry.

7

Preparations

Robert took charge of the situation. He took one look at Great-Aunt Marion, realised who she was and how she must be feeling, and introduced himself.

'Good evening. I'm Robert Weston and I met Moth at Covent Garden. She told me that she was worried about coming home by herself, so as I live in this direction too, I offered to see her safely home.'

Great-Aunt Marion was too much of a lady to show her feelings to a stranger. Besides, she was suspicious of young men with long hair. But as he didn't seem to have done Moth any harm and meant well, she thanked him and then marched Moth off into the rainy dark.

Nothing was said on the way home and yet the silence was frightening. Moth was also, she realised, very hungry. Her great-aunt must have known this, because a hot drink and biscuits came before the lecture. It was all about responsibility. About how her great-aunt was responsible for Moth while she was away from her parents, and how it was Moth's responsibility to behave properly and not be deceitful. Moth hated the sound of this word and tried not to listen any more because it made her feel so guilty, but she couldn't shut out the warning that any more deceit would mean straight home and no more ballet school.

And yet when she got to bed she was so tired that even the thought of being sent home in disgrace didn't keep her awake.

Her great-aunt didn't refer to the matter again, and Moth was glad that she wasn't a person who sulked or bore a grudge. There was enough to cope with at school, what with end of term exams, the project on *La Fille*, which somehow Moth didn't enjoy, and the preparations for the Christmas show.

Although the main show took place at the end of the summer term, when all sorts of agents and talent-spotters were invited, the parents liked and expected something at Christmas. But Mrs. Fraser firmly refused to stage yet another Nativity play.

'I insist on a rest from kings and shepherds and hordes of wretched angels,' she said at a staff meeting. 'And I'm sure Mrs. George must be fed up with those everlasting wings which looked very tatty last year.'

It was agreed, however, that there must be some Christian theme, so it was decided to recite and mime 'The Ballad of St. Christopher', which tells the story of a huge giant who used to carry travellers across a deep river on his back, and who one day ferried across a little boy who turned out to be the Christ child. One of the seniors was chosen to play the giant and much to his fury Tom, as the smallest boy in the school, was told that he was to be the Christ child. He minded very much about his lack of inches and hated playing a part that emphasised this, but apart from scowling and looking gloomy there was nothing he could do about it. And his mother, of course, was delighted.

Selsey saw the Christmas show as a wonderful chance for her to shine. She hated being in the background and told everyone that she felt she should do a dance number on her own. Her class was the despair of Miss Pearson, who complained that she couldn't even do a plié properly. She was also hopeless at keeping time with the rest of the class, but instead of being ashamed, she managed to imply that everyone else was in the wrong.

'Of course they won't let you do a solo,' said Jane. 'You're about the worst dancer in the class and you haven't passed any exams.'

'Who cares about silly little exams,' drawled Selsey, trying to annoy Jane. 'I'm a star and everyone wants to see me. I'm the only person here who's been in films and you're lucky to have me here.'

And so it seemed. Because when the programme was pinned up on the notice-board, Selsey was down for a solo tap dance.

Like everyone else Moth was puzzled – after all it was a ballet school and the only other soloist was Marina, the girl Moth had disturbed on her first day – but she was glad not to be in Selsey's shoes. Moth still felt nervous about dancing in front of an audience, and her part as one of the berries in the Christmas garland ballet was enough for her. Each class made up a part of the garland of holly and mistletoe, with the dancers in red, green, and tinsel costumes and Marina a lone figure in white.

'The effect,' promised Miss Pearson, 'will be stunning, if you can only get it right.'

Each class learnt their steps separately, and then during the last week when exams were over the whole school was given over to preparing for the show. Moth was also in the choir and sang carols until her head rang with glorias and ding-dong merrily on highs. Little Miss Ellison drilled the choir mercilessly while Russell Watson thundered away on the piano, and even he began to flag as his fingers plodded through yet another chorus of 'Here we come a-wassailing'.

When she was not dancing or singing, Moth was sewing buttons and press clips on the stack of clothes being run up by Mrs. George and her helpers. The seniors cut out and machined the costumes under her direction while Moth and the other juniors, who were not so reliable with the sewing machines, had to do all the fiddly things that had to be done by hand.

'We never hire anything. We make everything ourselves' was Mrs. George's motto, and whenever she said this, which was all too often, Jane would whisper 'More's the pity'. She hated sewing even more than Moth did, and was so careless that she put a row of press clips on the wrong side.

'What a stupid little girl you are,' said Mrs. George unsympathetically. 'You'd better do unpicking instead.' And she unloaded on to Jane a heavy costume that reeked of mothballs because it had been in a trunk so long, and told her to unpick the red lining which was needed for one of the holly berries.

Although the berries did only a short simple dance, Moth liked the rehearsals most of all. They took place in the studio-theatre and were the nearest she had come to appearing on a real stage. As each class was taking part in the ballet, she had a chance to watch the older dancers at work and see how the various dances fitted together. The atmosphere was an intoxicating blend of hard work and excitement. There was music all the time. Either from Russell Watson, who had written special Christmas music with clever echoes of carols, or from a tape recorder which did duty for him when he was needed elsewhere.

Dancers cast off sweaters and leg-warmers, did a few pliés or stretched in careless arabesques, put on point shoes, tried out steps off and on stage, asked for their music again, and yet again. Miss Pearson sat in the third row and kept leaping up on to the stage to re-position a dancer or show them just what she had in mind. Each dance showed off the level of a particular class, and they all came together in the finale to compose the garland. Moth found the greatest problem was not doing the right steps but arriving in the right place at the right time.

'Let's have some smiles,' implored Miss Pearson, as a grimly serious troupe of holly berries scattered across the stage, 'you look as though you were attending an execution. And I said smile not leer,' she added, as the berries made a ferocious effort to look happy.

Tom, as a reward for submitting to the part of the Christ child, had steps that exploited his gift for leaps and somersaults, and shot round the stage like a firework, becoming a real menace after he'd heard one of the seniors say, 'That little kid's very good'.

The only people in the whole school who seemed immune to the magic of rehearsals were Selsey and

Marina. And they had much in common. Both hated waiting for their turn and expected to have the stage to themselves. Both were armed with cassettes of their music and preferred to practice in secret. Both were cut off from the others in their class: Selsey because everyone was fed up with her showing off and Marina because she was so intense. So Moth didn't see either of them dance until the actual performance.

She was particularly looking forward to her father coming to the show because she wanted him to understand why dancing was so important to her. Surely if he saw someone as good as Marina he would realise that it wasn't a game but a proper career.

The day before he telephoned to say that he wouldn't be able to get away in time. 'I'm sorry love, but it's turned out to be an important meeting with a chap from head office and I can't leave early.'

'But you promised,' wailed Moth. 'You promised you'd see me dance.'

'And I will one day. You know I'd much rather be watching you than stuck in the office, but it can't be helped. Anyway, we'll all be thinking of you and you must tell me all about it.'

Moth put the phone down and sighed. Why were offices so much more important than people, at least to her father? Her great-aunt was coming to the show, so there would be someone who belonged to her, but her father was special and no one could take his place.

8

The Christmas Show

The show took place on the evening of the last day of term. School finished at midday, and that morning classrooms were either empty or taken over by odd groups trying to sort out last-minute changes to a step or movement. And they were furious at being interrupted.

'Can't you find somewhere else,' said a senior crossly when Moth and Ruth came to collect some books from their desks. 'Come back later. We must get this dance worked out and the stage is tied up all morning.'

They crept away. Officially they were meant to ask Mrs. George if she needed a hand with any more sewing, but both of them felt they couldn't face another press clip. There was a final choir practice after break, but until then they decided to play hide and seek, which seemed to match the party feeling of the day.

'We can't use the whole building,' said Ruth sensibly. 'It would take too long and you might never find me. Let's stick to the rooms on this side of the hall.'

Apart from Miss Lambert's study, which neither of them would have dared to hide in, this meant the library, various classrooms, an odd little waiting room which was sometimes used as a sick room, the art room, the old kitchen, and some dusty rooms at the very top of the house where no one ever went.

Ruth hid first, and after a ten-minute search that seemed more like an hour Moth was ready to call the whole thing off. The rooms right at the top, which had seemed so inviting, scared her. They were full of a jumble of old stage equipment and the faded flats of earlier shows that flaked paint if you so much as breathed on them. Moth felt sure they housed spiders too, and she couldn't imagine that Ruth would want to risk being approached by them as she crouched among the musty relics.

She drew a blank in the library and found the art room occupied by a couple of scene painters putting the finishing touches to the props for St. Christopher. They had no time for children playing games. She was about to pass the little waiting room that led to the principal's study when it struck her that although it didn't offer much scope for hiding places, Ruth might think it daring to be so near the lion's den and count on Moth not having the courage to look round.

The door was shut and Moth had to nerve herself to turn the handle and go in. The room seemed to be empty, but the door leading to the study was ajar. Moth tiptoed across to look behind the settee, the only obvious hiding place in the room, and then stopped at the sound of ugly sobbing. It came from the study and was interrupted by the calm voice of Miss Lambert, who was obviously trying to quell the tears.

'I understand how you feel, my dear, but is anything

going to be solved by your withdrawing from the Christmas show? You asked me to let you show the others what you can do, and I agreed because I appreciate that this term has not been easy for you. After enjoying the limelight you've had to take a back seat and discover that there are many things you can't do as well as the others. I know you've been criticised and resented it, but this isn't a school for budding film stars but for dancers who are being trained for careers that will mean a lot of hard work and perhaps not very much glamour.'

'Nobody likes me,' said a voice that Moth recognised, though it was very unlike the confident way in which Selsey usually spoke. 'But at least they all knew that I was a star. Now they'll all laugh at me when they hear that the film has been cancelled, and they'll be glad. It's in all the papers,' she added with a sob.

'I doubt if anyone here has had much time to read the papers today,' said Miss Lambert gently. 'I suspect they're all much too busy. And as you're not coming back next term, you won't have to face them then. But it's too late to change the programme for tonight. The audience will be expecting to see you, and they'll remember you for the wrong reason if you don't appear. You're going back home and I'm sure you'll get another part before long, so why not leave us on a brave note. Go ahead with your dance and prove that you believe in the old stage tradition that the show must go on whatever has happened to those taking part.'

Moth had not been able to stop herself listening. She knew it was wrong to eavesdrop on private conversations and that she had no right to be there, but a terrible excitement, a longing to know what happened next, had rooted her to the spot. But now the spell was broken and she slipped quickly out of the room, not quite closing the door after her in case the slightest sound should rouse Miss Lambert.

She still hadn't found Ruth, but she no longer wanted to go on with the game. She had never liked silly Selsey and thought it was ridiculous for her to be playing a child ballerina when she couldn't do the most simple exercises properly, but she saw what a blow it must have been when the film fell through. And she was surprised to find that she felt sorry for her.

Suddenly she remembered the choir practice and scampered across the hall to the music room, where a harassed Mr. Watson was trying to cope with the excited gestures of Miss Ellison, who was determined to get her crescendos perfect. She was just in time to take her place next to Ruth and there was no chance for talking until afterwards.

'Wherever did you get to?' said Ruth, when they had finally carolled the last Gloria in excelsis to Miss Ellison's satisfaction and were making their way to the cloakroom. 'I waited ages for you and then Jane came in and asked me to a secret meeting.'

'What was the secret?'

'It's about Selsey. Everyone's fed up with her showing off and going on about being so famous, so Jane suggested that we should do something to mess up her precious dance. She thinks we should put some of that gum she's always chewing on her tap shoes, so that she sticks to the floor, and Drew thinks we should put dried peas in them so that they hurt.'

'But she'd notice that when she put them on,' said Moth. 'I think the whole idea is silly, anyway. Let her show off if she wants to.'

Ruth looked surprised and hurt. 'All right,' she said, 'I won't tell you what we decided after all. I thought you'd enjoy the joke instead of being so stuck up about it.'

And she walked off, leaving Moth with something else to worry about. Should she warn Selsey?

Moth worried all the afternoon about what to do. She thought of asking her great-aunt's advice but guessed what it would be: that Moth should tell someone about the plan and protect Selsey by getting the others into trouble. She knew that she couldn't do this but decided that she would find out where Selsey was changing and then stay by her to stop anyone meddling with her things.

Her form were to change in their classroom and then file over to the studio just before the performance began. Selsey had not arrived and as the minutes wore on Moth began to think that she had decided not to dance after all. But at twenty-five past seven Selsey appeared. She had changed at home and looked like a miniature Fred Astaire, with a top hat, white tie and tails. Instead of trousers she was wearing black fishnet stockings, and her show biz glamour made a striking contrast with the demure charm of the holly berries in their scarlet tutus with matching headbands and pale tights. Ruth and Jane giggled but Selsey took no notice of them and looked scornfully at Moth as she changed places so that she could carry out her self-appointed mission. From the looks of the others she guessed that they had some plan in mind.

Each group remained in their seats until just before their item was due. There wasn't much room offstage and it was necessary to move very quietly. Selsey's tap shoes would have made this impossible, so she was carrying them and was to put them on in the wings. When it was her turn, she bent down to pick up her shoes but couldn't seem to find them in the dark. There were murmurs of 'shsh' as she scrabbled about on the floor, and at first Moth thought that hiding them was the plan, but then they were passed up from the end of the row. Selsey seized them and Moth sensed that no one was disappointed. Everything, it seemed, was going according to plan. But what could they have done to the shoes in the dark? And then suddenly she knew the answer. None of them had any pockets for carrying dried peas or anything similar, but there was one very simple place in which to carry something destructive: in one's mouth.

Moth got up and pushed her way along the row muttering 'Sorry, must go to the loo'. There were several in the corridor leading backstage and she rushed down it looking for Selsey. She was not in sight, but she had parked her unmistakeable tap shoes on a chair in the wings, perhaps while she too went to the loo.

Moth picked them up and looked at the soles: they were covered with blobs of chewing gum. She managed to drag most of it off, but suddenly Selsey was beside her. She snatched the shoes away and said accusingly, 'What are you doing to my shoes?'

There was no time to reply and nothing to say, for at that moment the boy who was stage managing came up to check that Selsey was ready and hissed, 'Shut up. You're on in a minute'.

Moth sped back to her seat and was in time to see Selsey come on. Some of the parents had seen her on the screen, and the whole audience was curious to see such a pint-sized personality at first-hand. Selsey sensed their interest and it spurred her on. Her song and dance act was an imitation of something far beyond her years. She was aping a nostalgic adult glamour, pretending to be one of the great stars of Hollywood, and she would have been laughable but for her personality. She believed in herself. She believed that she was fun to watch, and the brashness that made her so unbearable offstage enabled her to sparkle in front of the footlights.

It was the kind of act that Moth herself found creepy, but she knew it had taken courage to go on. The audience saw only the person on stage and that was what mattered; they applauded not only her dancing but her sheer vitality.

There were more carols, and St. Christopher, with a radiant Tom perched on the giant's back, and then came the garland finale. Moth was too dazzled to see into the darkness beyond the footlights but she could feel hundreds of eyes. It was quite different from dancing for an audition. On stage she felt as though she had stepped into another atmosphere, was breathing pure oxygen. She wanted it to last for ever. She wanted to transfix the audience so that they couldn't go home, so that she could stay in that small square of light where all her movements had a purpose and where she was conscious not only of the need to shape her steps to the music but of being part of the design that moved around her.

Each class added to the garland: red and white berries, light and dark green leaves, gold and silver tinsel, and finally Marina, a simple figure in white. Crowded in the wings as she waited to come on for the final grouping, Moth watched Marina's solo and knew why she wanted to be a dancer. The steps were so matched to the music that they seemed to unfold it and Marina danced with a confidence that lifted dancing above mere steps. She made it look so easy that when it was Moth's turn to run on and help form a bouquet around the centre of spinning whiteness, she felt that the whole secret of dancing was there in front of her, that she could reach out and catch it.

The applause was tremendous. There were flowers for Marina and Miss Lambert, who made a speech thanking everyone for all their hard work. Then dancers flowed over into the audience, looking for parents and friends, while a distraught Mrs. George made frantic appeals for everyone to get changed first and not to fling their costumes down anywhere.

Moth recognised Great-Aunt Marion's white hair and edged towards her, anxious to avoiding meeting up with Selsey. Then she saw that her great-aunt was not alone but talking to a familiar figure. She launched herself on her mother in a wave of delight while Toby and Lynette capered round her.

'I saw you, I saw you,' chanted Lynette, her eyes shining with pride, and Moth felt as though she had been running an obstacle race of feelings and only now reached her goal.

'We only decided to come at the last minute,' said her mother, laughing at Moth's surprise, 'and as we weren't sure whether the car would make it in time, I told Marion to keep it a secret. She's very good at keeping secrets, as you'll find out.'

'Why, is there another one?' said Moth, hoping that her father would suddenly appear.

'Yes,' said her mother, 'there's a really big secret, but this isn't the place to tell you. Go and get changed and then we can go back to Marion's and she can tell you all about it.'

9

The Awful Secret

Moth thought about the secret all the time she was changing. What could it be? She tried to work out what she would like best in the world and decided that it would be for her father to get a job in London, so that they could all live together again. Perhaps this was it. Or perhaps they had won top prize on the premium bonds.

It was a family game to plan what they would do if their number ever came up, the sort of house they would live in, how they would have a pony and a boat. Mrs. Graham also wanted a holiday in a really luxurious hotel where she would be waited on hand and foot and not have to plan meals and do all the shopping and cooking and washing. They felt quite guilty when she spoke like this, but then she would laugh and tell them not to be silly. She enjoyed looking after them and she loved cooking. It was doing it all the time that got her down because it didn't leave her much time to be a person in her own right.

Moth was rather alarmed at the thought that her mother wanted to be someone different; she loved her just the way she was. But as she struggled out of her tutu and took off her ballet shoes she decided that the secret couldn't be anything as drastic as that. Her mother's expression had been teasing rather than transformed.

She bumped into Ruth as she made her way into the hall; their quarrel of that morning seemed forgotten.

'Have a super Christmas,' said Ruth. 'Perhaps you can come to tea in the holidays and see my things.'

'I'd love to if I'm back in time,' said Moth, overjoyed by the way in which the future was suddenly opening up and promising to be more fun.

She squashed into the back of the car with Toby and Lyn. Toby had been very impressed by Tom's antics. He and Drew had done a tumbling dance of whirling leaps and somersaults and Toby envied their lightning speed. He wanted to know if they played football.

'I expect so,' said Moth, 'though we don't do it at school. I know Tom has a skateboard and he's much better at it than you are.'

'You haven't seen me for ages,' protested Toby indignantly. 'I can crouch right down now with one leg out and no hands.'

'So can Tom.'

'Bet he can't. Bet you wouldn't know a christie if you saw one.' And Toby began to press her against the side of the door, reinforcing his argument with his familiar strong-arm tactics. Moth prepared to fight back.

'Stop it, you two,' said her mother. 'You've no idea how tiresome children can be,' she said to Great-Aunt Marion. 'These two are always squabbling and competing, and it nearly always ends in blows.'

Great-Aunt Marion smiled. 'I seem to remember that

my brothers were much the same. They always wanted to be bigger and stronger and better at everything than me. I spent hours one summer jumping to and fro over the washing line because I did so want to be best at something.'

'And were you?' asked Moth, trying to imagine her great-aunt sailing over the high jump.

'Yes, but it didn't last long. They soon had even longer legs and I could only beat the younger ones.'

By now they were back at the flat where Great-Aunt Marion had prepared what she called 'a high supper'. Even Toby was impressed by the food, but the gracious setting didn't prevent him from tucking in.

There were rolls of ham speared with gherkins, sausage rolls hot from the oven, marmite twiglets, two flavours of crisps (to which Moth had introduced her), bowls of nuts, and little squares of brown bread topped with smoked salmon and a twist of lemon.

'What's that funny pink stuff?' said Toby suspiciously, and then had to be restrained from making a pig of himself when he discovered that he liked the salty tang of the salmon.

Lynette sat contentedly munching a sausage roll and blowing bubbles through her straw while Moth suddenly realised how hungry all the excitement had made her.

'What's the great secret?' she said, crunching her way through the crisps.

'Well, I think Great-Aunt Marion should tell you,' said her mother. 'It's really her secret.'

Great-Aunt Marion took a sip of her drink and the amber liquid caught the light and sparkled like a jewel. 'It was my idea,' she began, 'and perhaps I should have talked it over with you first, but I didn't want you to be disappointed if it didn't work out. You see it's worried me that you've had to be so much on your own. I'm not much company for someone of your age and I thought you might be so much happier if you had someone of your own age here.'

Moth wondered whether she ought to apologise for not having seemed happier.

'As you know, two of my brothers went out to live in Australia, and when I wrote to Jack about Moth he told me that his granddaughter Libby was very keen on dancing too and having lessons. Libby's mother was killed in a car crash a few years ago, and ever since she's been living with her grandparents. I gather from Jack that they find her rather a handful at times, and as she hasn't any brothers or sisters I think she's missing a lot. Her father is a pilot with Quantas airlines, so he would be able to come to London and see her sometimes, and he agrees that it would be lovely for her to join a real family, especially as you're both so keen on dancing.'

Great-Aunt Marion paused to take another sip of sherry; she was obviously very proud of her secret. 'Libby will be arriving here after Christmas, and I've arranged for her to go to school with you next term. You'll be able to look after her and show her the ropes, and I'm sure you'll have lots of fun sharing a room and being able to talk about your dancing.'

There was silence. Everyone was waiting for Moth to say something.

'Well, Moth,' said her mother at last, when the silence had become embarrassing, 'don't you think it's a good idea?'

'No, I don't. I think it's a rotten idea. I don't want some horrid Australian round my neck. You might have asked me first.'

'Moth,' said her mother, 'stop this at once. How dare you talk to your great-aunt like that.'

'How dare she make plans behind my back,' shouted Moth. 'I never complained about being on my own. I never asked for some awful cousin to come poking her nose in here. I don't want her and I won't help her. She can find her own way to school, just like I did. I hate her. And I hate all of you.'

And Moth rushed out of the room and ran up the stairs to her bedroom. She slammed the door and used all her strength to turn the big old-fashioned key. Then she flung herself down on the bed and gave way to choking sobs.

After a while she turned over on her back and looked round the room. In the last couple of months she had become very attached to it. The drawers of the green leather desk were full of her possessions, her ballet post-cards were arranged on one wall, the little white book-case was gradually filling up with her library of paper-backs, and high up on the sloping wall Anthony Dowell looked down in shadowy grandeur.

It was the only room Moth had ever had all to herself, and although she missed the family, the room had some-how consoled her and seemed a symbol of growing up, of the independent life she was slowly learning to make for herself. Now this pride of possession was to be shattered. The room would have to be shared – and with a complete stranger. The future, which had begun to look so much more promising after a term of trial, was now uncertain and upset and the joy of seeing the family had been changed into the misery of a row.

Moth hoped that her mother would come upstairs and rattle the door. She longed to let her in and explain why she had been so angry. But no one came. From below came sounds of clearing away, then noises in the kitchen, footsteps in the hall, and silence. Presumably Mrs. Graham and the children had been stowed away on camp beds and settees.

Moth was too exhausted to cry any more or to get undressed. She lay there listening for her mother until eventually she fell asleep.

10

Home Again

Moth was very subdued on the journey home. She sat in the back of the car with Lynette and hardly spoke. Nothing further had been said about Libby at breakfast and her great-aunt had said a cool goodbye that seemed more disappointed than angry.

They stopped for lunch at an American ice-cream parlour that also sold giant hot dogs. Toby managed to eat two smothered in ketchup and relish and then spent ages weighing up the merits of thirty-two different flavours of ice-cream. He narrowed the choice down to toffee, coconut, blueberry, or New York butter pecan, and finally decided on the latter because he wanted to try pecan nuts. Moth just pointed to the nearest one, a garish green with chips of almond in it, and couldn't remember afterwards what the taste was.

She had often looked forward to going home, but as the car drove under the arch of the old town wall and past the historic Market Cross, now stranded in a sea of parked cars, she felt no thrill at the sight of familiar shops and streets. Her temper had worn her out. She felt faded by crying and as though she had become a pale person without the strength to feel anything any more.

She also had a headache, and by the time they arrived home it was so bad that she had to lie down. It was strange being in such a small bedroom again. Her half looked unnaturally tidy, with her books put away, her dolls stacked in a forlorn row, and her bear looking lost in the expanse of her bed. She was too old for him but had refused to hand him over to Lyn and now she was glad to see him.

It was too dark to see much of the garden, though the lights from downstairs spilled over onto the lawn. The swishing of the wind sounded like waves and the windows were panes of ice. Moth touched them with her cheek and savoured the wildness outside from the warm security within.

She left the curtain open and lay on her bed. Rain began to sting the windows and as she listened to the wind in the dark the pain in her head slowly eased. She heard the front door bang and knew that her father had come home. She hoped he would come up to her, but he went into the living room and she pictured him sitting in front of the fire. The smell of fried sausages drifted upstairs.

Moth saw herself as too ill to eat, but as the smell became stronger and richer and she remembered the crispness of her mother's chips, she had second thoughts. She hadn't eaten much all day and suddenly she felt hungry.

As she stood outside the kitchen door she wondered for a moment if she still belonged. Then she went in to light and warmth. Toby was supposed to be laying the table, there was a hiss of frying from the cooker where her mother was juggling with the plates, Lyn was grizzling with impatience and her father was sitting at the table orchestrating the confusion.

'We're all in our places with bright smiling faces,' he chanted, swinging Lyn up from the floor and planting her firmly on a chair. 'Hullo,' to Moth, 'you decided to join us?'

Moth nodded and sat down in her old place. Toby had given her a huge fork and a small knife but he hadn't forgotten her mug. Everything was gloriously the same, except for some new drawings by Lyn which included a spidery 'My Daddy'. When her mother set down a dish of fat sausages (two and a half each and four for her father) Moth knew she was home.

After they had all helped with the washing up, Mrs. Graham put Lyn to bed and Toby shut himself in his room to work on a Christmas secret. Moth and her father sat in front of the fire.

The Grahams still had a proper coal fire, though Mrs. Graham complained, half-heartedly, about the amount of extra work it made. Moth loved the uneven patterns of the firelight and the occasional pieces of live coal that flared and spluttered with untapped energy. She saw that her mother had remembered to buy some chestnuts as a winter treat, and her father took out a handful and began to slit the shells with his penknife.

'Sorry I missed seeing you as a red berry,' he said. 'Even Toby was impressed. Promise I'll come next time, even if it means missing the most important conference of the year.'

He picked up the shovel, arranged the chestnuts on it, and then balanced it carefully between two slabs of coal. The orange ashes flared up, scorching the underneath of the shovel.

'I gather there were a few fireworks afterwards, though. And that instead of being pleased that your cousin is coming to join you, you staged one of your tantrums and were very rude to your great-aunt.'

Moth was silent. The split in the chestnut shells was

widening and she could see the white kernels beginning to turn a pale yellow.

'It's too late to put her off, you know,' said her father. 'And it's going to be much worse for her. She's already had to cope with losing her mother, and now she's being sent halfway round the world to a country where everything will be strange and new. I expect you've made some friends at school, but she'll be the new girl who comes in in the middle of everything. Even if your dancing is much the same all over the world, she's bound to do some things differently. You know now what it's like to be homesick, so what do you think it will be like for her?'

Moth tried to imagine. She pictured someone with one of those Australian accents people laughed at. Someone who would share her room and see all her things. Someone who would be there for every meal and perhaps be nicer to her great-aunt. Someone who would want to sit next to her at school and walk home with her every day, just when she was making friends with Ruth. And, said a voice inside her head, perhaps she'll be someone who can dance better than you, who'll get all the attention and sympathy because she hasn't a mother and is far from home, who'll . . . But Moth made the voice stop. It was also telling her that she was mean, whereas her father was asking her to be generous.

I can't help it, I can't help it, she thought. I bet he wouldn't like it if someone new turned up at his office and he had to share everything with them.

The chestnuts were now splintering and turning black. Her father put the shovel in the hearth to cool and looked for an old *Radio Times* to put the shells on. He didn't press Moth for an answer.

'Give it time,' he said. 'Wait and see what she's like. You may be in for a pleasant surprise.'

He put his arm round Moth and she snuggled against him and watched the fiery turrets topple and disintegrate.

A few minutes later Toby switched on the light and said indignantly, 'Hey, you've been roasting chestnuts. That's not fair. I want some.'

He bounced across the room and Moth sat up and began to do battle for the charred heap that was now cool enough to eat.

11

Opposites

Christmas went in a flash. One moment it seemed as though it would never come. More and more cards arrived. There were whispered conferences about presents. Mrs. Graham ticked her way through endless shopping lists. There was the usual argument about whether to have a real Christmas tree or a plastic one and the usual frantic search for last year's decorations. Then in a glorious rush of opening stockings and presents and eating too much it was all over.

Great-Aunt Marion gave Moth a record of Prokofiev's music for the ballet *Romeo and Juliet* and a promise to take Moth to see it the next time it was on in London. 'And this time we'll get the tickets in good time,' she wrote on her card. Moth was still at the stage of being a little wary of music she didn't know. Once she had a tune to hold on to or felt that she could dance to the music, it was all right, but she tended to get lost or even bored without some guidelines. But the bold dramatic music was as exciting as Tchaikovsky (her favourite composer) and when she heard the lovers' theme she knew that she must dance Juliet one day.

She was surprised to find out how much she was looking forward to going back to school. She felt that she wanted to get on with life instead of just marking time at home. Her former best friend came to tea but there wasn't much to talk about any more, now they went to different schools and had new friends. Jenny still went to the same dancing classes, but she seemed to recognise that Moth had outgrown them.

Increasingly Moth felt that she was suffering from what her granny called 'the hump'. This was the way you felt when you had nothing to do, it was pouring with rain, and you didn't want to read, paint, play records, or finish a jigsaw.

'I shall be glad when you've gone back,' said Mrs. Graham when Moth had made Lyn cry yet again by being too bossy. Toby was no help either. He had been given a huge box of old stamps, many of them still stuck on scraps of envelope, and he spent hours in the bathroom soaking them off and leaving the washbasin full of soggy paper.

Moth had managed to forget Libby, but as she and her father drove back to London the thought of her cousin loomed up and even spoilt the pleasure of having her father all to herself. He told her about Great-Aunt Marion's brothers, whom he had known when he was a small boy.

'They were both in the navy during the war,' he said, 'and I can remember being terribly impressed when they were home on leave. And I was rather frightened of cousin Rex, Libby's father. He was older than me and used to play the most awful practical jokes. He once got me into the cupboard under the stairs by pretending that he'd invented some marvellous new light. Then he shut the door and left me there in the dark.'

'Were you frightened?'

'Terrified. I howled so loudly that someone soon came and let me out – and Rex was in disgrace afterwards.'

Moth wondered if Libby would take after her father. 'I shan't let her frighten me,' she thought.

To their surprise Libby had already arrived. She had flown in with her father, who had breezed across London, scooped up Great-Aunt Marion and taken her out for a slap-up meal.

'Rex is so full of life,' she told them. 'He insisted on taking us to one of those restaurants where you help yourself by carving off huge joints of meat. I told him I had a small appetite, but he carved me a great plate of roast lamb, then some roast pork, and after we'd eaten enough meat for a family for a week, he went back again and got himself a great plate of roast beef. He must cost a fortune to feed,' she said with a laugh, turning to Libby.

'Sure, Dad likes his food,' agreed Libby with a grin. She had grey eyes, short wavy hair, and a suntan that was miles away from an English winter. Unlike Moth, she didn't seem at all shy and was brimming over with the excitement of the past few days.

'I've seen Big Ben and the Houses of Parliament, and Buckingham Palace and Nelson's Column, and had a ride on the Underground, and seen the soldiers who wear those big black fur hats, and . . .'

Great-Aunt Marion and David Graham both laughed.

'I can see she's been keeping you busy,' he said.

'Yes, but I've loved it. If you live in London all your life you take these things for granted. You know they're there and you tell yourself that you'll have a look at them one of these days, but it takes someone like Libby to make you realise how exciting London is. Do you know after all these years I've never been to see the Changing of the Guard. Until yesterday.'

'That's true,' said Mr. Graham. 'And I'm delighted that Libby's so keen. I hope you'll now have two enthusiasts on your hands, and I only hope you won't find them too exhausting.'

'Well, I don't think my legs are up to walking miles, but I have promised Libby the Tower of London and a trip down the river when the weather's better. And I've been thinking about some of the things you and Rex and Patrick liked doing when you were young. Do you remember being taken to Pollock's and all buying toy theatres?'

'What's Pollock's, Daddy?' asked Moth. She had been feeling very out of the conversation and guilty about not having been more interested in London. She remembered that her great-aunt had wanted to take her sightseeing but she hadn't shared Libby's enthusiasm.

'Pollock's,' said her father, 'was a very old shop that sold toy theatres that you could make yourself. They were all based on real theatres that had existed years ago, and you got not only a cardboard model of the theatre but the text of some bloodthirsty play and all the scenery and characters to go with it. I remember I spent hours cutting them out and Patrick was very keen on the Penny

Plain ones that you had to colour yourself.'

'Did they only cost a penny in those days?' said Moth disbelievingly.

'Well they did originally, when they were first printed, but not by the time I bought them. The first ones were sold for a penny plain and twopence coloured, and this expression became famous. I'm surprised that Pollock's is still going. Are you sure?'

'Yes,' said Great-Aunt Marion. 'As soon as I remembered the name I looked them up in the phone book and rang up, and apparently they still sell toy theatres and now have a toy museum. So I thought we might add it to the list of sights.'

'When can we go?' said Libby impatiently. 'Is it open tomorrow?'

'You're certainly going to have your hands full with this one,' said Mr. Graham, exchanging amused smiles with Great-Aunt Marion, 'I only wish I could help out, but it's time I was getting back. Libby must come and stay with us in the holidays and put my lot to shame with her enthusiasm. I don't think they know much about where we live, though it does have quite a history.'

Moth couldn't be bothered to protest. She went downstairs with her father to say a private goodbye. The earlier greyness of the day had turned to rain and the streetlights gained brilliance from the liquid pavement.

'She's not at all as I thought she'd be,' she said quietly. 'She doesn't seem at all homesick and she's awfully pushy.'

Her father pulled her hair playfully. 'I like her, and I think she'll be good for you,' he said. 'You could do with a little more push yourself.'

Moth hugged him reproachfully and then shivered as she watched the car turn the corner. And it was not on account of the chill damp. Perhaps he was right. She was still uncertain about so many things, above all about herself and her ability, but the last thing she felt she needed was a confident cousin who didn't look as though she had a nerve in her.

Then she remembered the shared room. She had meant to sort out her treasures and put the more private ones away. What had Libby done to them? She rushed upstairs and flung open the bedroom door. The room was in darkness apart from the reflections on the ceiling. There was no sign of Libby or of a second bed.

She could hear voices in the kitchen as she went down to join them. Her great-aunt had started the washing up and Libby was helping. She was telling her great-aunt about a fabulous beach picnic her friends had arranged as a goodbye party.

'Where am I going to sleep?' said Moth abruptly, breaking into Libby's account of sun-bathing on Christmas Day.

'In your room, as usual,' said her great-aunt, groping with her rubber gloves for the last spoon.

'What about Libby?'

'She's got her own room,' said Great-Aunt Marion, smiling at Moth as though they shared a private joke. 'I decided that you were quite right about the room. It isn't really big enough for two. So I cleared out the other attic, and although Libby has to share her room with a few old trunks and odds and ends she doesn't seem to mind.'

Moth was surprised to find that she was both relieved

and disappointed. She had made up her mind to put up with her cousin, to swallow her down like some nasty medicine. Now it seemed there was no need. She could keep her room all to herself. No one asked her to be a martyr.

As she went back upstairs to start unpacking, she thought how unsettling it was that nothing ever turned out to be quite as you expected.

12

'Twopence Coloured'

Libby longed for it to snow because it never did at home, except in the mountains, but the weather refused to oblige and just went on sulkily raining. The damp tweaked at Great-Aunt Marion's arthritis, and she put off any more sight-seeing until there was only one day left before term began.

'Please,' begged Libby, 'please can we go to Pollock's tomorrow? If we don't go then, we shall have to go on a Saturday when there'll be lots more people. And you said it just isn't a place for crowds.'

The next day was as damp and grey as ever, but Great-Aunt Marion gave in. Pollock's turned out to be on the corner of a row of faded houses quaintly squashed together. On one side someone had painted a mock shop window and high up on the brickwork above, the painted figure of Harlequin was springing up to the sill of another false window. Moth noticed that even the real windows were crooked, and slanted as though they had been drawn in by a child.

Libby had run ahead of them and was pressing her

nose against the shop window. The chill mist outside made the small bright room look comforting and cosy. It was a jumble of drawers, trays and boxes spilling over with puppets, models, cutouts, and an assortment of miniatures from minute potted plants for dolls' houses to tiny tables laid with miniscule plates and cutlery.

The entrance to the toy museum was through a door inside the shop. The assistant explained that it was two small houses joined together and that you went up the stairs of one house and down the stairs of the other. Moth felt as though they had suddenly stepped into a giant doll's house and been reduced to miniatures themselves. The narrow stairs twisted sharply and the rooms were small and had sloping ceilings and uneven floors. On every side were displayed the leftovers of childhood, the toys and games of children who were probably now as old as Great-Aunt Marion.

Although Moth and Libby both felt that they were too old for dolls and doll's houses, they looked at them to please their great-aunt, who was not too old to enjoy them. The French dolls had kept their beautiful pale complexions and had soft curling hair, shining eyes fringed with real lashes, and delicately painted eyebrows. Their clothes were trimmed with lace and had rows of tiny buttons that must have taken ages to undo. They looked rather vain, and Moth noticed that one of them had her own mirror and comb, and a proper garden-party hat trimmed with faded organdie.

What she liked best was the room with the bears. There were two that were more than seventy years old, and they looked their age. Moth felt sorry for one sitting in a chair who was trying, she felt, not to look up too often at a painting of his much younger self which showed him as a much more sprightly bear. His stuffing had shifted, giving him a lumpy stomach, and he was stitched and bald and only fit for retirement. He made Moth feel that she must be a little kinder to her bear when she went home. It was sad to be neglected just because someone had grown too old for you.

Libby wanted to know how old the houses were. She had always lived in a modern house in a modern city and she was very impressed by the age of everything in London. 'How many hundred years?' she asked Great-Aunt Marion, who said she thought the houses had probably been built in the eighteenth century.

They saw the toy theatres that Uncle Patrick had loved, and just as their fathers had done they clamoured to buy one. They found the books with the cardboard models in the shop, and Moth couldn't decide whether she wanted the Victoria Theatre with *Cinderella* or the Regency Theatre with *The Sleeping Beauty*. Her great-aunt suggested that they should each have a different one, but they both wavered over who was to have what.

They were busy comparing the scenery when Moth was startled by an amused voice that said, 'I think you're more of a Cinderella myself. I should have that one.'

It was Robert, looking like a character in a melodrama with his vast greatcoat and a long striped scarf wound round and round his neck.

Just then Great-Aunt Marion came out of the other room saying that she had found enough presents to last her for the rest of her birthdays and Christmasses, and Robert was introduced to Libby.

'It's a pleasure to meet you,' he said gallantly, 'but I'm

afraid I can't stay because Morris is sitting on a yellow line. I've just called in to pick up a new play. But I'd be happy to give you all a lift home, especially as it's such a foul day.'

So they bought one Victoria and one Regency and hurried off to rescue Robert's car. It was dark now and as they waited while Robert folded down the front seat and threw his junk into a corner of the back, Moth looked back at the shop and thought how easy it was to believe that you could step inside and into the past.

*

Robert was asked to tea and he proved a great help in getting the theatres assembled. Libby wanted to start on hers as soon as they got home and pestered her great-aunt for scissors and sharp knives and glue before she had had time to put the kettle on.

'Surely it'll wait a few minutes,' she protested as Libby overturned her sewing box in search of another pair of scissors. Moth had bagged the first pair and was already cutting out the stage of her theatre under Robert's direction.

'I'm hopeless at doing things myself,' he said, stretching out on the floor and propping himself up on one of the best flowered cushions, 'but very good at telling other people what to do.'

Moth bent the edges of the stage under and tucked the corners round and glued them together. Robert volunteered to hold them in place until the glue worked. Then she started cutting out the proscenium arch. This went round the front of the stage and bore a splendid coat of arms and lots of ornamental twirls. The gilt boxes on either side of the stage were hung with swags of red velvet and in one of them a man with a monocle was quizzing the stage. The people in the boxes reminded Moth of her visit to Covent Garden, though none of the people there had worn such grand clothes. It was tricky cutting round the row of footlights and along the fringe of the looped-up curtain and Moth was glad when her great-aunt brought in tea.

She had made a stack of toast and there were two kinds of jam and Marmite for Moth, who much preferred savoury toast.

Robert was obviously a jam man, and just as he was

about to bite into a slice laden with fruit Libby asked him what he did and why he had been buying a play at Pollock's.

Moth was too shy to ask him. She guessed that he didn't work in an office because he didn't dress or talk like her father.

Robert finished his toast and helped himself to another piece before replying. 'I'm a student,' he said.

'A student of what?'

'Well, life, really. But officially I'm supposed to spend my days in the Reading Room of the British Museum, sending for piles of books, making lots of notes, and eventually, I suppose, writing a book myself.'

'What'll the book be about?' said Libby.

'The theatre. In the nineteenth century. In fact about the very kind of theatres you're busy making. Which is why I know about Pollock's. I used to go there when I was a schoolboy, and it was playing about with model theatres that started my interest in theatre history.'

'Do you get paid money for playing with toy theatres?' said Libby, who was shamelessly inquisitive.

Robert laughed. 'Yes and no. I've got a grant to write my thesis, and so far I've managed to persuade the authorities that I'm working very hard. But I expect they'll find me out some day and then I shall have to work like everyone else.'

'I expect you work very hard,' said Great-Aunt Marion reprovingly. She didn't really approve of modern students, but she liked Robert and was determined to think well of him.

After tea they got down to the theatres in earnest. Robert and Great-Aunt Marion read the instructions aloud and held corners in place. Moth and Libby wielded the scissors and were sometimes in such a haste that they chopped off odd corners and even vital parts. But by supper time there were two resplendent theatres with stout columns at the four corners and sturdy wings with slits to take the scenery.

'My fingers won't cut any more,' said Libby, throwing the torturing scissors down. 'We'll have to do the characters tomorrow.'

'Wouldn't it be lovely to dance on a stage like this?' said Moth, putting her theatre on the sideboard and kneeling down to look into the stage. 'It would make a beautiful setting for a ballet.'

'Diaghilev had the same idea,' said Robert, and added proudly, 'and I bet not many people could tell you that.'

'What did he do?'

'Went to Mr. Pollock's shop, just like you did, and fell in love with the old engravings of the pantomime characters. Then when he wanted to commission a new ballet, which he was always doing, he suddenly remembered the old prints and decided that he would build a ballet round them.'

'Can we go and see it?' said Libby.

'Heavens, no. It was staged a long time ago and everyone's forgotten about it by now, though you sometimes come across photographs of it. But Moth's right about the theatre. It would be a lovely setting for a ballet, so perhaps you should try and make one up.'

Libby looked doubtful, but Moth thought it was a lovely idea. She took her theatre up to bed with her and stood it on her chest of drawers. When she was in bed she switched off her bedside lamp and got out the torch she kept under her pillow. She had always had one there since the days when she was very small and afraid of the dark. Now she switched it on and directed the beam on to the empty stage, moving it round as though it were a spotlight. The theatre looked more alive by torchlight, and the stage was so inviting that Moth longed to step on to it.

'That's the sort of theatre I shall dance in one day,' she said to herself. And then she fell asleep.

13

Tom's Challenge

To Moth's surprise and slight dismay, Libby soon proved to be the most promising dancer in their class. She was well proportioned, relaxed, and had had a good teacher, and Miss Pearson was delighted with her.

As she had done Cecchetti examinations in Australia, she fitted into the class without any trouble and like the rest of them was soon hard at work on Grade 4.

It involved various exercises such as pliés and battements at the barre, and then port de bras and more battements in the centre. In the adage, the slow movements section, there were grands ronds de jambe en l'air with an arabesque, and Moth tried to think of her poster of Makarova, who didn't look as though she ever wobbled. Libby was very good at pirouettes and at the different jumps, the changements, echappés, temps levés and jetés. In the final part of the examination they had to do a sequence made up by the examiner and then a dance of their own. The dance had to be no longer than a minute, but Moth felt sure that it would be one of the longest minutes of her life. They ended the examination, like all their classes, with a bow or a curtsey, which was considered a polite way of thanking the teacher or examiner.

There was always a break after class in which they changed out of their tights and leotards. The school was too small to have a uniform, but Miss Lambert made it very plain that she didn't approve of jeans and even Drew, who carried his possessions in a curious ex-army haversack, managed to conform as far as wearing grey flannels.

Break was the first chance to swap news, because Miss Pearson made everyone work so hard that there was no time for talking. Moth and Ruth liked to chatter away in the shelter of an old wall in one corner of the playground. It was near the few trees left, which had been carefully preserved in neat squares cut out of the asphalt. Moth had expected Libby to join them, but she much preferred the company of Tom, who shared her restless energy. He, in turn, liked her enough to tell her about his great problem.

His way to and from school lay past the local comprehensive school, a vast untidy complex of buildings that took up the whole of one street. Somehow some of the boys who went there had found out that Tom went to the Fortune School of Dancing, and they let him know just what they thought of it.

'Mind you don't get a ladder in yer tights.'

'Made yer fortune yet?'

' 'oo's afraid of football?'

Sometimes they would come along in a gang, boys who were all taller than him although about the same age, and walk close to him, so close that they were treading on his heels. He would try not to hurry, but then they would start to jostle him until his fear of being attacked got the better of him and his walk became a run and he would hare off up the road while the boys laughed and called insults after him.

He was afraid to tell his mother. He knew that she would insist on coming down to the boys' school and making a fuss, and then they would have something else to jeer at. He knew that dancing wasn't sissy, that it required far more strength and muscle than most of the boys who made fun of him possessed, but how could he make them see that? Their heroes were footballers, and although Tom had heard of a football team that had tried ballet exercises and found them quite exhausting, this wasn't the sort of thing you could explain in the street.

He began to think of his day as having two danger zones, two periods that had to be lived through somehow. He worked out that it didn't take more than five minutes to walk past the school, and he told himself that five minutes really wasn't very long. There were ways of getting through the danger zone. Sometimes when he turned the corner there was someone else coming along. An elderly lady coming back from the library. A mother with a toddler in a push chair. Tom would tag along just behind them and use them as a kind of smokescreen. He knew that the boys wouldn't attack him when anyone was about. Their bullying was a private war.

Libby was the only person he confided in. She shared his indignation but felt that they must fight back.

'I bet they're not good at anything,' she said. 'I bet

none of them could jump as high as you or turn cartwheels as fast as you can.'

Tom was flattered and comforted by her admiration. But it didn't do much practical good.

'Lots of grownups feel like they do,' he said. 'My grandfather is always making awful jokes about me turning into a little swan. *Swan Lake* is the only ballet he's ever heard of, and he thinks it's terrible that I should be doing girls' stuff.'

But, ironically, it was Tom's grandfather who gave Libby the idea of a way in which Tom could show his persecutors that dancing was for real boys. For Tom's eleventh birthday he gave him a complete skateboard outfit: board, crash helmet and knee pads. The present was meant as a challenge: a challenge to Tom's mother, whom he thought was to blame for all this ballet nonsense, and a challenge to Tom to show that he really was a normal boy.

Tom's mother was furious. She didn't realise that Tom already owned a rather battered skateboard and she saw the present as a dangerous threat. 'Tom could have a very nasty accident and ruin his chances of dancing for ever. It's a most unsuitable present for a child in his position, and I insist that you take it back.'

But Tom's grandfather was a wily old man. He loved his grandson and wanted to be proud of him, but he saw nothing to be proud of in a boy who wanted to dress up in fancy clothes and jig round a stage. It wasn't his idea of being manly, and he was sure it was all the fault of Tom's mother. He winked at Tom, packed the present up, and then when his mother was out of the room told him that he could keep it if he was prepared to hide it away.

'But where?' Tom asked Libby. 'My mother would find it wherever I put it. She's always dusting and poking about in my room.'

'Why not give it to me,' suggested Libby. 'My bedroom's already got lots of things stored in it. I could easily hide the things behind one of the trunks and then we could share them.'

Tom brought his present to school in instalments and Libby managed to take them home without even Moth finding out. Moth and Ruth liked to dawdle on the way home, whereas from now on Libby and Tom raced back. Libby would tell her great-aunt that she was going out to play with Tom, smuggle their gear downstairs, and then they would scoot off looking for a suitable slope.

If Great-Aunt Marion was at all surprised, she wasn't over curious. She was pleased that Moth and Libby had found their own friends, and as long as they were not too late for tea, she looked forward to a quiet time with her library book.

Libby and Tom had a marvellous time experimenting with the skateboard. They both had a natural sense of balance and were fearless. Their ballet training had taught them to relax, and although they kept falling off they were soon inventing all kinds of variations, mostly thought up by Libby.

The competition was her idea too. It came to her when Tom arrived very late for class and couldn't put a foot right. He told her afterwards that he had been set on by a couple of boys who had snatched his case, emptied it out, and made fun of his practice clothes.

'They pretended to dance round in them and then

threw everything all over the place,' he said, almost crying with anger. 'It took me ages to find everything and I knew Miss Pearson would be furious if anything was missing.'

'Never mind,' said Libby consolingly, 'they only do it because it makes them feel stronger than you. But they're not, not really. I bet they can't skateboard half as well as you.'

And then she had her idea.

'Why don't you challenge them to a skateboard competition? You could show them once and for all that dancers aren't cowards or sissies.'

14

Out of Control

It proved surprisingly easy to provoke the boys to a contest when they next came across Tom on his way home and started their familiar jostling.

'D'you like fairy stories?' asked one of them, a skinny boy with a tee shirt featuring a monster-like gorilla. 'Read fairy stories, do you?'

The others laughed as though the Beast had made a brilliant joke. One of them bumped into Tom and trod heavily on his foot.

'Sorry,' he said with mock politeness, 'hope I haven't hurt yer twinkletoes.'

'That's a good name for 'im,' said one of the others, 'little Fairy Twinkletoes.' And they all began to chant 'Fairy Twinkletoes, Fairy Twinkletoes'.

Tom felt sick. In desperation he looked down the road, hoping that some woman would come along so that he could walk close behind her. He was sure that the boys wouldn't actually attack him in the presence of an adult. But the street was empty and the cheerful spring sunlight flooding the road seemed to mock him.

One of the boys had a skateboard and was shunting along on it. Tom remembered Libby's challenge and wished she was there to support him.

'Bet you can't do a handstand on that,' he said. He had meant to say it in an offhand assured way, but his voice sounded shrill and unsteady.

'Hark at Twinkletoes,' jeered the Beast. 'Fancies himself on wheels. Does Mummy let you play with nasty dangerous wheels?'

Tom flushed at the mention of his mother. 'If you think you're so good,' he said, 'prove it. Let's have a contest to see who's really afraid.'

The boys starting chanting 'Twinkletoes on wheels, the garden gnome on wheels,' but the Beast was considering.

'Right,' he said, 'yer on. Know the ramp outside David Morgan? We'll see you there on Thursday after school. You can show us how well you can dance, little fairy.'

And with that the gang lost interest in Tom and ran off down the street, jumping up here and there to strip the branches of young leaves just venturing out.

Tom told Libby what had happened the next day and was comforted by her enthusiasm. 'We'll show them,' she said.

Both she and Tom were determined to master a christie by Thursday. This involved crouching down on the board with one leg sticking out in front and both arms stretched out to balance. Libby fell off several times and grazed her hand and knees. She had a stoical disregard for knocks, even when they brought tears to her eyes, but Great Aunt Marion was far more upset.

'What have you been doing?' she said when Libby arrived home with grubby handkerchiefs round her knees. 'These cuts must be bathed at once and properly disinfected.' And she made Libby sit still while she bathed her knees and hand with hot water and then applied antiseptic cream. 'You can get an infection very easily,' she said, swabbing out the pieces of grit.

'You can get lockjaw,' said Moth cheerfully. 'Perhaps you'd better keep your mouth open all the time so that it doesn't get stuck.'

'Don't be silly,' said her great-aunt crossly. 'There's no need to worry as long as you disinfect cuts properly and make sure there aren't any splinters in them.'

Great-Aunt Marion had done a First Aid course during the war, and Moth could imagine her being marvellous in a crisis because she was so cool and unfussy. But her calm was shattered when Libby developed a sore throat and a streaming nose.

'Back to bed with you, my child,' she said firmly after Libby had picked at her breakfast and mopped her way through half a box of paper tissues.

'I must go to school,' protested Libby, struggling to find the energy to defy a cold and her great-aunt.

'Nonsense. Moth can explain, and I'm sure they won't want you spreading your germs all round the school.'

Libby gave in only after a promise that she could go tomorrow *if* she was better, but when Moth came home in the afternoon she found Libby much worse and obviously destined for several days in bed.

Her face was flushed, she had a temperature, and her chest wheezed like a concertina.

Moth tried to reassure her that she wasn't missing

much, but as soon as Great-Aunt Marion had gone downstairs Libby told her about Tom and the contest.

'If he doesn't turn up, the others will think it's because he's afraid, and then they'll tease him even more. And it'll be all my fault because it was my idea in the first place.'

Her hoarse voice was painfully urgent and her flushed cheeks and bright eyes disturbed Moth.

'You'll have to take the board in tomorrow,' she said. 'I've hidden it under that big bush in the front garden.'

Moth was appalled. She hated her brother's skate-board and the whole beastly craze, and she remembered that they had all been warned in their first term of the injuries it could cause.

'If you don't,' croaked Libby, 'I shall get up and take it myself, when Great-Aunt Marion isn't looking.'

Moth knew she meant it.

'All right,' she said miserably, 'I'll do it.'

David Morgan House was a block of flats called after one of the local councillors. It was part of an estate that had been designed with some thought for the people who had to live there, and the various blocks were linked by concrete gardens with square patches of grass and oblong flower beds. The gardens were at different levels and were joined together by steps and ramps that were ideal for boarding. There was also a dismal sunken basin that had started out as a pond but had been drained when all the fish disappeared and several toddlers fell in. It had gradually filled up with rubbish and dead leaves until one of the boys on the estate had seen a film about boarding and realised its potential. Cleaned out it wasn't quite up to a Hollywood swimming pool, but the sloping sides had their moments.

There was a raw March wind blowing on Thursday and Moth dug her chin well down into her scarf which was wound several times round her neck. She would like to have disappeared right inside it so that she was invisible, because she so wished that she hadn't felt obliged to turn up with Tom. But he had obviously been relying on Libby for moral as well as practical support.

The Beast was wearing a bomber jacket and jeans. The jacket zip was broken and another lurid disaster, this time featuring a car chase, was stencilled across his shirt. Moth was afraid of him and his friends. There was a casual violence about them, about the way in which they moved in a pack, kicking at anything that got in their way and viciously grabbing any trees and bushes that crossed their path. One of them had found an old can and kept hurling it against a wall. The jangling crash seemed to amuse him but suddenly he tired of the game and leapt on the can, using his full weight to crush it as he might have crushed an enemy.

'Brought our girlfriend, 'ave we?' said one of them, eyeing Moth.

'Well she's not 'is mother,' said another. And they all laughed as though they had only one laugh between them.

'Right, let's go.' The Beast shot forward on his board and flipped down on to the next level of the gardens. Tom shunted along behind him and Moth followed them, trying to pretend that she just happened to be passing. When they got to the empty basin the Beast began to ride up the curve of the sides, flicking the board round in a turn as he reached the top.

Tom watched the Beast's technique. He and Libby had not found anywhere like this to practise, but he was used to copying an exercise and his agility and sense of balance, sharpened for a very different purpose, stood him in good stead. He rattled down one side and shot up

the other, matching the Beast's speed and daring.

The Beast was unimpressed. He jumped out of the basin and zig-zagged through the gardens, dodging round the cutouts of spring green grass and beds spiked with roses. Tom pursued him, angling his body so that his board rolled and bucked obediently. Finally they came to a longer slope where a ramp wound down to the street. The Beast crouched down until he was lying across the board and his body seemed to graze the paving as it spun past.

'Let's see yer handstand,' he called up as he clattered to a standstill in the middle of his gang.

Tom gripped the ends of his board, launched it with two or three steps and then kicked his legs up and locked his elbows. His body was poised vertically over the board and the watching boys were impressed.

'Magic,' said one admiringly.

The board gathered speed and at that moment a large mongrel came bounding up the ramp.

'Tom, look out,' shouted Moth, but her warning was too late. Tom swerved to avoid the dog but had no time to cartwheel upright. The board bounced off the side wall of the ramp and Tom thudded down on to the pavement.

The boys scattered at the scent of trouble leaving Moth and the dog alone with Tom. He was obviously hurt, but Moth couldn't tell how badly because Tom didn't say. He just lay there on the ground without moving.

15

Taking the Blame

Although it was only a few seconds it seemed an eternity to Moth before Tom opened his eyes. In the meantime the dog licked him, decided he was not something to eat, looked hopefully at Moth, and then ambled away.

Moth knelt down and tried to see where Tom was hurt. There wasn't any blood as far as she could see but she was frightened by his stillness. Supposing he was dead? People did die from being hit on the head. How would she know? Just then Tom made a noise, a whimper of pain that increased as he tried to turn his head.

Moth wondered whether she should help him to sit up. She had an idea that you weren't supposed to move people after an accident in case it made them worse. And weren't you supposed to keep them warm? Perhaps she should put her raincoat round Tom. She looked desperately round the gardens to see if anyone had noticed them. The Beast and his gang obviously didn't want to be mixed up in any trouble and although Moth was surrounded by flats their windows looked down on her like blank faces that just didn't want to know.

Tom sat up and didn't seem sure where he was. Then he tried to stand up and his eyes filled with fear and tears.

'My foot hurts,' he sobbed. 'It feels all funny and as though it won't hold me up. How am I ever going to get home?'

Moth knew that he was trying hard not to cry but the pain and the uncertainty about what had happened to his foot were too much for him. She knew that when she was ill the one person she wanted was her mother and it occurred to her that Tom might feel the same.

'Do you think I should phone your mother?' she asked. 'Perhaps she would come and take you home.'

Tom didn't know. His head ached, his foot throbbed, and he couldn't cope with the voices calling him a coward and his mother fussing and worrying about his career. He wanted someone to come along and take care of everything and he left the decision to Moth.

The best thing was obviously to send for help, but Moth couldn't find a phone box that worked. The one outside David Morgan had been wrecked in style – even the instructions had gone – and it seemed to be the only one for miles. When she approached a passer-by, the woman looked at her suspiciously and muttered something about trying the shops. There was a parade further down the road and although there was no sign of a phone box, one of the shops was a sweet-shop-cum-paper-shop-cum-post-office.

Moth rushed in, looked wildly for a phone, and burst into tears.

The woman behind the counter had just reached the most exciting moment in a romantic thriller and was not pleased at being disturbed. 'What's the matter with you?' she said crossly.

'It's Tom. He's hurt his ankle and he can't walk. I must get in touch with his mother and I can't find a phone anywhere.'

'Well,' said the woman more sympathetically, 'there aren't many public ones round here, but seeing as it's an emergency, you can use mine if you like.'

She lifted up a flap in the counter and led Moth into the back of the shop. It was dark and small and stacked with bundles of newspapers and magazines and cardboard boxes. They were full of bars of chocolate, but Moth had never felt less tempted by sweets. She wouldn't have wanted them even as a gift. She remembered the rather overbearing woman who had brought Tom to school that first day and shivered at the thought of having to tell Mrs. Blundell-Smith that her darling had been injured.

Nothing was easy. It took Moth ages to find the number – did one look under Blundell or Smith? – and then she wasn't much good at explaining where they were. In the end Mrs. Blundell-Smith had to say 'Some place called David Morgan' and leave it to the taxi driver. Then Moth led her to Tom. She had propped him up against a wall and covered him with her raincoat, and he looked like a forlorn guy. There was a huge bump on the back of his head and his face was smudged with tears and dirt.

'My poor little treasure,' said Mrs. Blundell-Smith, smothering Tom in her arms. 'Whatever's happened to my poor boy?' Moth was glad that no one else was about to hear these endearments but Tom was too upset to care.

He limped along between his mother and Moth and winced every time his left foot touched the ground. His mother was entirely concerned about him. She helped him tenderly into the taxi, told the driver her address, and drove off without a word of thanks to Moth. The whole affair, Moth saw when she looked at her watch, had only lasted about an hour; she wouldn't even be very late for tea.

As she hurried home she wondered what would happen next. Tom's mother would be sure to find out about the skateboard and make a terrific fuss, but that she herself might be blamed in some way was something that never occurred to Moth.

Tom wasn't at school next day and Great-Aunt Marion insisted on keeping Libby at home. Moth just had time to tell her that Tom had been hurt before Great-Aunt Marion insisted on a game of snakes and ladders. As Moth slithered down a particularly evil-looking snake she reflected that life was just like that. Things seemed to be going well and you got on and then, wham: you landed on a snake and had to go right back to the beginning.

Her real-life snake turned out to be Miss Lambert, who summoned Moth to her study.

'Sit down, Jennifer,' she said, looking across her desk in a way that made Moth feel very small. 'I understand you're a friend of Tom Blundell-Smith.'

Moth nodded. She hated being called 'Jennifer' which she never thought of as her real name. It was a proper name, shared by lots of other people, where 'Moth' was special and belonged just to her.

She hadn't spoken to Miss Lambert since her interview and found her rather frightening. She couldn't reconcile her plain appearance with the pretty girl in photographs of the days when Miss Lambert had taken her orders from Marie Rambert, Ninette de Valois and Sir Fred himself.

'I think you know that Tom had an accident last night, but perhaps you don't know that he's broken his ankle.'

Moth was shocked.

'His mother is keeping him at home for a few days and of course he won't be able to dance again for at least a couple of months. Mrs. Blundell-Smith is very upset because it seems that the accident was caused by a skateboard that she had forbidden him to use and thought had been given away. She tells me that in fact he gave it to you and that you encouraged him to go on using it although you had been warned that it was dangerous.'

Moth was stunned. There had been some mistake. It was Libby not she who had encouraged Tom. She hadn't known anything about it. She tried to think of some way of explaining what had really happened without getting Libby into trouble, but Miss Lambert swept on, taking Moth's silence as an admission of guilt.

'I would like to remind you,' she said sternly, 'that unlike most schools we are not obliged to keep any pupils here. As I told you at your interview, there are lots of reasons why pupils are sometimes asked to leave. Usually they are reasons outside their control, but they all add up to the one most important reason: because the staff and I have come to the conclusion that they won't make dancers.

'One of the most important qualities a dancer needs is the ability to benefit from advice. If you ignore it and think that you know best, then you're not likely to do well at something that requires discipline above all else. Some of the rules may seem a little harsh, but I'm sure you know why you are advised not to do certain sports or take risks that would harm other children, don't you?'

Moth nodded. She wanted to say that it was unfair. That she didn't break rules. That it was all Libby's fault. But the words wouldn't come. Miss Lambert had made up her mind.

'I've spoken to some of the staff and they are very surprised that you have behaved in this silly way. But it's more than silly, because your disobedience might have resulted in the end of another pupil's career. And that is something I take very seriously. If your parents were in London I should want to discuss the matter with them, but I have decided not to involve them at this stage. Instead I shall keep a special eye on you in the future. If you do well in examinations and your conduct is satisfactory, then all will be well. But if you show that you are not ready to accept the school rules then I shall have to tell your parents that you would be better off in an ordinary school.'

Moth left the study with the same relief with which she got down from the dentist's chair. The most important thing was that it was over, and she felt like a prisoner who had suddenly been set free. But then on the way home she was filled with resentment against Libby. She had never wanted her to come in the first place and now she might even take Moth's precious chance away from her.

Moth ran upstairs determined to make Libby promise to explain the situation to Miss Lambert, but her room was empty. She was angry. Angry with her great-aunt for interfering. Angry with Miss Lambert for never doubting that Moth was to blame. Angry with Libby for preferring the company of Tom and causing so much trouble. It wasn't fair. It wasn't fair.

She felt sorry for herself and she looked round the room for some way of getting back at Libby. Her eyes fell on Libby's theatre and in a spiteful rage she knocked it off the chest of drawers and stamped on it. Her foot crashed down on the triumphant arch, the stiff curtain, the sets and actors, the footlights, and the theatre crumpled under her onslaught and became a heap of torn and bent cardboard.

Moth knelt down and pulled at the pieces, but even all

the king's horses and all the king's men couldn't have put them together again. The theatre was broken beyond repair and the only thing left to do was hide the remains. She pushed them hurriedly down the back of the chest of drawers, wondering whether Libby might possibly think that the theatre had mysteriously slipped down there of its own accord.

Then she went down to tea.

She found Libby telling her great-aunt about the ballets she had seen in Sydney and the parts she was hoping to dance one day.

'When I'm older and have finished my training,' she confided, 'I shall go back home and become the prima ballerina of the Australian Ballet. I shall practise and practise until I'm world famous and people will come to Australia just to see me.'

'Isn't that rather a tall order?' said Great-Aunt Marion, smiling at Moth. 'If you're so famous you'll be asked to dance in all the great opera houses and you won't be content to stay in Australia.'

'Yes I will,' said Libby firmly, 'because I want everyone to see how good the Australian company is. I get so fed up with everyone over here going on and on about the Royal Ballet. I bet they're not really all that good.'

It was Moth's cue to start an argument, but to her great-aunt's surprise she seemed miles away. She was wondering whether to tell the prospective prima ballerina that first she would have to own up to breaking the rules. Perhaps Miss Lambert would then threaten to send her away. She was certainly far more likely to do something else wrong before very long. And did Moth really want her to go? She wasn't sure.

So while Libby prattled on about Marilyn Rowe and Michela Kirkaldie and Gary Norman, the current stars of the Australian Ballet, Moth made a pact with herself. It wasn't so much a pact as a bargain, a case of if I do this then that will happen. The bargain was: if I don't tell on Libby, in exchange please let me pass all my exams. It was a deal with Fate, like holding your collar when you see an ambulance, but it made Moth feel much better and she ate a large tea.

16

Sea-break

For much of the spring term it had been grey, cold and wet, the sort of weather when it seemed right to be indoors working hard, but it was in the summer term that work reached its climax. Moth and Libby felt so restless that they actually enjoyed the exhausting routine of class, but it was one thing to fling oneself into jetés and pirouettes and another to concentrate on maps and sums and French verbs when the trees outside were shouting a very different message.

Libby never stopped complaining about being miles from the sea and having to make-do with a small overcrowded swimming pool. She went on and on about how marvellous it was back home until Moth began to picture Australia as one vast swimming pool fringed by sandy beaches creamed by surf. She herself didn't like swimming much because she so hated those first moments when the water explored you with icy fingers.

'Why can't we go to the sea, just for the day?' Libby pestered Great-Aunt Marion. 'It's so near London. Back home we drive fifty miles just to find an extra good beach.' She was being what Moth's father, after several weeks of Libby during the holidays, had dubbed 'irrepressible'. Lyn, who loved long words but didn't always get them right, had seized on this and kept saying that Libby was so pressable, which made Toby and Moth laugh.

'It's such a performance and so expensive,' said Great-Aunt Marion defensively. 'If we had a car it would be different. I'm afraid you'll just have to make the most of the swimming baths.'

So Moth went on shivering down the steps and dipping in the shallow end while Libby plunged down length after length like a young dolphin.

The baths shared a building with the library, and one day they bumped into Robert, who had tickets for libraries all over London. Libby immediately told him how many lengths she'd swum and how it wasn't an Olympic-size pool and how cramped and shut in London was.

'You sound as though you could do with a day by the sea,' said Robert sympathetically. 'I know just how you feel. The BM is all right once you get into the Reading Room, but there are so many tourists that it takes ages for them to check you in, and if I have to stand on the steps too long I start thinking that it's much too nice a day to spend inside with a lot of books that will wait until a rainy day.'

Moth thought that he was only agreeing with Libby out of politeness, because he was surely old enough to have joined the ranks of grown-ups like her father who thought that it was one's duty to go to work however tempting the day. But she was wrong about Robert.

A few days later he rang up Great-Aunt Marion and suggested that they should all go to the sea on Sunday in his Morris.

'I thought somewhere not too far just in case Morris is taken short,' he explained, 'but I think Southend would be a fairly safe bet.'

Libby wanted to know all about Southend.

'It's years since I've been there,' said her great-aunt, 'and I expect it's all changed, but it used to be a great favourite of Londoners and it's got the longest pier in the world.'

'What's a pier?'

'A way of walking on the sea without getting your feet wet.' But she refused to tell Libby any more and answered every question with 'Wait and see'.

Morris seemed to have got the message that much was expected of him, and once they were through the traffic of the East End they chugged along at what Great-Aunt Marion thought was a very nice speed and Robert confessed was about Morris's limit.

Moth and Libby shared the back seat with a splendid hamper they had found in Great-Aunt Marion's collection of things-not-to-be-thrown-away-because-they-are-bound-to-come-in-useful-some-day. Her idea of a picnic sounded more like a banquet, with cold chicken, boxes and boxes of unusual salads, iced soup, real coffee and, as a special treat, early strawberries. She arranged everything so properly that Moth was sure they were taking a tablecloth, too.

Libby was determined to be the first to see the sea. But as the car turned down towards the sea front and they came out onto the road that overlooked the estuary and across to the further shore she was strangely silent.

'Where is it?' she said at last in a subdued voice. 'That's not the sea!'

Moth saw what she meant. The shore was littered with a galaxy of small boats, most of them belonging to local fishermen, but instead of bobbing about on the water they were perched in flatlands of grey mud. The tide was out, and so far out that it had left behind a vast foreshore to the delight of boys in wellingtons who were digging furiously for bait.

Robert laughed and then tried to soothe Libby's disappointment. 'I'm sorry. I should have checked the tide times and warned you. But it comes in very quickly once it's turned and we'll go out to the end of the pier and find the sea.'

The setting for the picnic was less elegant than Great-Aunt Marion would have liked, but at least Robert found somewhere full of interest. They perched on a wall at the top of the beach like a row of hungry gulls, and while Great-Aunt Marion unpacked the hamper and fussed over the iced soup (which was a delicious concoction of tomatoes, onions, green peppers and cucumber), Robert pointed out the landmarks and swept the horizon with his binoculars. He enjoyed ship-spotting and told them about the liners, oil tankers and cargo boats that turned off the high seas at this point and came past on their way up the estuary to the docks at Tilbury. He told Libby about cockles and Southend rock and promised her a sample, and he whetted their appetite for the narrow nautical highstreet at Leigh and the long streak of the pier.

Great-Aunt Marion said she didn't feel equal to tackling the pier, so after the picnic they drove along the front and found the perfect parking place for her and Morris, where she said they could keep each other company.

The sun was shining on the pier so that Moth felt they were walking along a causeway of light. Gulls screamed overhead and when they had got about halfway they caught up with the sea which was curling gently back towards the land. The town dwindled behind them and they seemed to be sailing away on the deck of a great liner.

On the journey down Moth had been thinking about the exam this week and the final verdict that lay on the far side of it. Everyone seemed to have their problems. Was Jane growing too tall, was Ruth getting too fat, would Tom's ankle be all right? Would Marina be the first pupil to get a place in the Royal Ballet's senior school, and who would win the prize for the most promising dancer in the first form? Moth was weighed down by anxieties but on the pier the breeze took hold of them and carried them off as lightly as a balloon. There was sea and sun and summer holidays ahead.

As usual, Libby wanted to see everything. They had to go into the shed where the lifeboat stood poised above the slipway ready to dash down into the water. They had to go right to the end of the pier and up some stairs to a little lookout hut where they hoisted signals when it was stormy. Then downstairs to the water where passengers still boarded ships amid girders encrusted with sea moss and tiny shelled animals.

'That's what piers were really for,' said Robert knowledgeably. 'To enable people to get on and off boats when the tide was a long way out. It's such a pity that nowadays going on a trip doesn't seem very exciting and so there are hardly any real passenger boats left.'

Libby was still very scornful of Robert's idea of the sea. The tide had turned now and the waves were hastening back but she was used to sea on a much grander scale, to the roar of surf instead of the very English murmur of lapping water. She longed to startle Robert and Moth and so she suddenly raced back along the pier shouting 'Bet you can't catch me.' And of course they couldn't.

Great-Aunt Marion was very glad to see them because it was very hot in Morris and she didn't approve of people who sat in their cars as though they were still at home and never stretched their legs. Unfortunately her legs didn't stretch too well because of arthritis and Moth longed to walk a little faster. Robert sensed her impatience and cheered her up by quoting in a whisper,

'"Will you walk a little faster?" said the whiting to the snail,
'"There's a porpoise close behind us, and he's treading on my tail."'

Libby loved the fishermen's stalls with their glistening harvest of pale pink shrimps and shiny black winkles and dolls' plates of cockles, and kept clamouring to try some. In the end Robert called for a truce in the shape of a proper seaside tea. They sat outside a café overlooking the sea, which was striding in now, and ordered cockles, winkles, shrimps (very fiddling things to eat, Robert warned), bread and butter, ice-cream, tea and fizzy drinks.

Moth loved the shrimps, Libby decided that the cockles tasted like fishy mackintosh, Robert admitted that he had an allergy to shellfish and it was left to Great-Aunt Marion to do the tea real justice. She said it reminded her of her school holidays when she and her brothers would spend their pocket money on plates of cockles drenched in vinegar. 'We were forbidden to eat between meals and of course this made them taste even better.'

All the boats were afloat now and the waves were nearly up to the pavement. Libby wanted to go for a swim but Great-Aunt Marion said firmly that they hadn't time to wait for her tea to go down. Libby sulked and then darted off to get her feet wet looking for shells. Moth refused to part with a very smelly piece of seaweed because she wanted to hang it up at home and see if it really would tell her when it was going to rain.

They played I Spy and car number spotting on the way back, and it wasn't until after Robert had dropped them at the flat and rattled off in Morris that Moth remembered that they weren't on holiday. Tomorrow was school and this was the week of the Cecchetti exam.

17

No Luck

One of Miss Pearson's firmest rules was 'No jewellery'. She didn't allow even the plainest necklace or bracelet in class – 'and I don't care if you were given it by your fairy godmother at your christening' – and when Selsey had protested against removing her lucky charm chain Miss Pearson had soon quelled her. 'No one, and I mean NO ONE, wears jewellery in my class,' she said, 'and if you wear that object again I shall confiscate it.'

Moth had heeded this warning and only worn the silver dancer her parents had given her at weekends and on her one visit to Covent Garden, when she had felt in special need of good luck and protection. It seemed to have worked, and so she wanted it with her during the exam. She knew that she couldn't wear the dancer round her neck, so she decided instead to tie it in her handkerchief and tuck that in her belt.

The sensible thing would have been to put it ready the night before, but Moth was too impetuous for that. She liked to leave everything until the last minute, and when her mother complained about this she said that getting ready in advance made her feel much more nervous.

So it wasn't until the morning of the exam that she started looking for the dancer. She had kept it in a number of places: in with her socks in the top drawer, under her pillow (when she was feeling extra worried), in one of the little drawers of the desk and, when she first discovered it, in the secret drawer which could only be opened by pressing a spring hidden under the ink well. It was only when she had searched all these places that she realised that the dancer was lost. But how, and where?

She was certain that she hadn't lost it outside the house, because she had always put it away very carefully after she had worn it and surely she would have noticed if it had been missing? And then she thought of Libby. She had never mentioned the theatre but she must have noticed that it had disappeared. Perhaps she had found the crumpled remains behind her chest of drawers and this was a silent way of getting her own back on Moth.

Moth didn't stop to think out her tactics. She barged into Libby's room and said furiously, 'Where's my dancer? Give it back to me.'

Libby was trying to find her best pair of tights, the ones without any darns in them. She looked up in surprise. 'What dancer? I don't know what you're talking about.'

'My lucky dancer. The one my parents gave me. It's on a silver chain and I wear it sometimes.'

'Oh, that one. I don't know where it is, I haven't got it.'

'You must have,' said Moth, getting desperate. 'You took it because I knocked over your theatre. I'm sorry, I didn't mean to break it. Not afterwards,' she added, more truthfully.

'So it was you,' said Libby scornfully. 'I guessed it must be. Great-Aunt Marion would have said if she'd done it, but then she doesn't creep round doing mean things.'

'Neither do I,' said Moth hotly. 'I didn't plan to do it beforehand and I've said I'm sorry. But you must have planned to take my dancer, and that's stealing.'

'I didn't take your silly dancer,' shouted Libby indignantly. 'If I'd wanted to injure you I'd have done it openly, in a fair fight. You're the one who does things behind people's backs.'

'I'm not, I'm not,' screamed Moth, and because there seemed to be no other way of getting the truth out of Libby she rushed across the room and began to shake her. Caught off balance, Libby fell on the bed pulling Moth down with her, and they struggled together like a pair of enraged kittens.

'What on earth's going on?' They had not heard Great-Aunt Marion coming upstairs. Moth and Libby let go of each other and stood up. They both looked dishevelled and angry.

'Moth's lost that dancer necklace of hers,' said Libby by way of an explanation, 'and she thinks I've got it.'

'Have you?'

'Of course not.'

'Right. Then pick up your things and get ready for school or you'll be late. Moth, go to your room.'

Moth went, and looked tearfully at the havoc caused by her search. She had flung things everywhere and all the drawers hung out in abandon. Her great-aunt finished despatching Libby, came in and shut the door.

'First of all,' she said firmly, 'you're going to tidy this room, and then you're going to tell me what all this is about.'

Moth obeyed, but she wasn't sure how best to explain the situation. She couldn't face telling her great-aunt that she had stamped on Libby's theatre in an earlier temper, but it was the main reason why she suspected Libby now.

'It's to do with luck,' she said lamely. 'I wanted to take my dancer to the exam with me because I thought she would bring me luck. I've got to pass the exam because if I don't Miss Lambert will make me leave. I haven't changed my mind about dancing, I love it more than ever . . . and I don't want to let Mummy down when she's working to give me a chance . . . Libby's all right but I don't want her to be here next year without me . . . ' Moth's explanation became more and more disjointed and brimming with tears.

Her great-aunt looked surprisingly sympathetic. She hadn't had time to put on her sensible daytime expression yet and she was still in a flowered dressing gown with her hair tied back in a simple plait.

'But why on earth should you fail?' she said. 'You're keen, you've worked hard, and you must be good at dancing or you wouldn't have got this far. Exams are for seeing how well you've done not for making you feel a failure. If you do your best you shouldn't need a lucky dancer or a lucky anything else to get you through.

'You know I used to be considered a very good judge of character when I was in the navy (Moth smiled, as she always did at the thought of her great-aunt in uniform), and I know you're going to do well. You've got it written all over you. The only trouble is that you waste so much energy on worrying about things that don't matter instead of forging ahead. If you really believed in yourself you wouldn't need any lucky charms.

'But you won't pass any exams if you don't get off to school, so you'd better get moving.'

Moth scrambled her things together. Libby had already gone. As she shot downstairs her great-aunt came out into the hall and said, 'Moth, I've just remembered. I found your dancer the other day when I was hoovering your room. It must have slipped down the side of your bed and somehow made its way underneath. I put it in a safe place, meaning to tell you, but it quite slipped my memory. Anyway you don't need it now. You'll only be worrying about losing it if you carry it around in your handkerchief. Don't forget, you need confidence not luck.'

Moth wasn't entirely convinced, but there was no time to argue. She would have to tell Libby, and apologize, and she was so late that she had to run all the way to school. But luck or not, she was extra careful not to step on any lines.

18

Honours Even

The summer show was a much grander and more serious affair than the end of term show at Christmas. For the leavers it was a kind of showcase designed to attract agents, scouts, and anyone who might possibly offer them a job. Some of them had already decided to become teachers, two were going to university, a boy called Inigo, who spent his time planning impossible stage sets and experimenting with lighting, was going to art school, a girl who had formed a modern dance group had won a scholarship to a way-out dance institute, two girls had been taken on by a minor German company and saw themselves as Marcia Haydée, and Marina, it was rumoured, was going to the Royal Ballet senior school.

For all of them the summer show was a glorious chance to show off before they became small fish in much larger pools, while for Miss Lambert and the rest of the staff the show was a chance to impress parents, old pupils, friends, critics, education authorities and those very special people who didn't look important but turned out to be millionaires looking for causes to support.

Although the whole production was mounted on a shoestring, the aim was elegance and sophistication. Mrs. George might be combing warehouses for seconds and leftovers, the cloak-rooms might be awash with exotic dyes and the sewing machines chattering late into the night, but come the great day the show must be perfect and seem effortless.

Moth's form were to start the evening with a light-hearted little ballet that made fun of the routine of class. Moth suspected that Miss Pearson had been inspired by memories of poor Selsey, who had found it so difficult to keep in step and always seemed to be on the wrong foot. Libby and Tom, whose ankle was now out of plaster and back to normal, were chosen to play the two children who couldn't put a foot right. Moth might have been jealous of Libby's star part but for the fact that she had actually been noticed by the intense Marina, who needed a junior in her ballet. The part was very small, but Moth was thrilled. To be honest, most of the time she sat in a corner watching, and Marina treated her like a slave and made her run errands and mind her shoes and leg-warmers and sweater, but Moth didn't mind. She would have done anything for Marina and resented it when Libby called her Marina's little lamb and taunted her with 'And everywhere that Marina went the lamb was sure to go.'

But then Libby had never felt the need for inspiration. She was restless and full of energy, and she danced as she ran and jumped and turned somersaults. Moth felt that she was surrounded by people who were much too practical and down to earth; she was attracted to dancing because it was bound up with very different feelings. Marina was the first person she had met who seemed to be aware of these feelings and to live in a world governed by them. She wasn't trying to pass exams or looking for a safe job. She danced because she had to, and Moth saw that because for her, dancing was another way of feeling, she had more than mere technical brilliance.

The show didn't begin until eight but beforehand there was a party for the most important guests. Moth and Libby were pressganged into helping Mrs. George, who had now changed her tune to 'We do all our own food.' They spent hours decorating squares of toast with smoked salmon and pâté topped with wisps of lemon and shiny olives, and stuffing little pastry cases with a delicious mixture of mushrooms and chicken. Moth couldn't resist helping herself and was quite relieved when Mrs. George banned any more sampling with the awful warning, 'You'll be sick, probably on stage.'

The party was held in the library, but the news that the most important guest had arrived soon reached the kitchen. She was, it seemed, someone legendary who had once danced with Nijinsky in the wonderful Diaghilev company. Jane said that she had also danced in front of the Tsar and Tsarina in their own special theatre in St. Petersburg and that Fokine himself had shown her how he wanted his steps performed. So *Les Sylphides* wasn't ballet history to her but a ballet that she had actually seen taking shape.

Moth was determined to set eyes on this fabulous being. She slipped out of the kitchen and along to the library, which was as crowded as a sardine tin. She pretended that she had come to fetch a plate and squeezed through the noise and smoke searching for someone who looked famous. The long windows were open and the party had spilled over into the garden which was perfumed with old roses. There was a seat by a bush massed with tiny flowers and someone was holding court there.

Perhaps because Jane had mentioned *Les Sylphides* Moth half-expected to see a figure in white muslin crowned with a circle of flowers. What she certainly didn't expect was a tiny old lady who was much much

older than her great-aunt. She was enveloped in a bizarre dress that sparkled as though it were jewelled and reached up to her bird-like face and down to her ankles. She was wearing soft ballet slippers and Moth saw that her feet were very small. Her eyes were still bright, but her face was creased as though it had been folded up and put away.

Moth stared at her, then remembered that it was rude to stare and turned away. She was bitterly disappointed. It seemed natural for someone like her great-aunt or her granny to be old, but it was only now that she understood that it happened to everyone, that even the most beautiful dancer in the world must one day grow old.

The realisation coloured the rest of the evening. It was so exciting that Moth wanted time to stand still, but it wouldn't. She saw that every minute she was moving into the future just as surely as those who were leaving.

Inigo had hidden floods and coloured lights in the trees and was impatient for it to get dark. He had worked out the most complicated lighting for one of the ballets, and after threatening to blow the fuse or electrocute himself he had become very calm and controlled and was now crouching in the darkness ready to switch on his master plan.

The first form ballet was a huge success. Tom's timing was so good and he tied himself up in such clever knots that a voice in front called him 'an infant Wayne Sleep' and Mrs. Blundell-Smith nearly burst with pride. Libby revealed an unexpected gift for acting, as the child who was longing to catch up with the rest of the class. When she finally managed to start on the right foot and do the right port de bras her delight was so evident that it drew a round of applause.

Then came a Spanish gipsy dance with lots of tambourines and castanets, and a hornpipe by all the boys with Tom as a very junior sailor. The third form did a mimed poem about a beautiful princess and her jealous suitors that ended up with everyone lying dead on the stage, and then two fifth formers acted the balcony scene from *Romeo and Juliet* with such passion that Mrs. Blundell-Smith made a mental note to ask Miss Lambert whether children should be made aware of these things quite so young.

Marina tried Moth's devotion by being at her most imperious. She insisted on sitting in a room by herself and expecting Moth to call her when it was her turn to dance.

So Moth had to hang around backstage and missed seeing *Kaleidoscope*, the modern dance ballet which was done to weird electronic sounds and disturbing patterns of light. Inigo was determined to impress a flamboyant Italian stage designer who was sitting in the front row, and to Inigo's joy he led the applause and kept shouting out 'Bravo'.

Marina seemed unaware of all the excitement. When it was time she picked her way through the tangle of ropes and wires in the wings, ignored Miss Pearson who was frantically trying to co-ordinate everyone, and electrified the audience. Moth had only a small part in the ballet, but she was so absorbed in watching Marina that she forgot to be nervous. As her mother said afterwards when they were talking about the highlights of the show, 'Moth was quite carried away. She looked so like a real dancer that I forgot I was watching my own daughter.'

The evening ended with a speech by Miss Lambert who came on stage looking transformed. She said that she was happy to report that the Fortune School had had

one of its most successful years and that parents would be delighted to know that former students were distinguishing themselves in many different fields. The current list included several teachers, a lawyer, two artists, a stage-designer, three stage-managers and four air hostesses. 'I like to think,' she said amid laughter, 'that ballet has its uses even up in the clouds.'

But of course the real aim of the school was to produce dancers, and it was encouraging that so many ex-pupils were finding places in companies, both at home and abroad. 'We haven't so far ever had anyone in the Royal Ballet, but having seen her dance this evening I know you won't be surprised to hear that Marina Guest has won a place in the Royal Ballet's senior school.' She had to stop because of the thunderous applause, and Moth couldn't resist giving Libby a 'told you so' look.

Then Miss Lambert went on to announce the examination results and Moth held her breath. Form One: Drew, Ruth, Jane and the others had all passed and were commended; then Tom Blundell-Smith, pass with Honours, Elizabeth Graham, pass with Honours, Jennifer Graham, pass with Honours.

Moth was so relieved that she didn't really mind when the prize for the most promising dancer in the first year was awarded to Elizabeth Graham. Libby received her prize from the handsome Italian designer, who spent some minutes talking to her and seemed much amused. When Moth asked her later why he had laughed, Libby said that she had told him that she came from Australia and that was where she had really learned to dance well.

In a way it was Libby's evening, because when they had sorted themselves out afterwards and met up with

Moth's parents and Great-Aunt Marion, Libby gave a whoop of joy and threw her arms round a suntanned figure in uniform. It was her father.

Lyn had already fallen in love with him because he was prepared to carry her on his shoulders – a feat that Mr. Graham prudently avoided – and Toby told Moth that Uncle Rex had promised to show him round his plane and let him sit in the captain's seat. Moth thought that Uncle Rex was just like Libby, all drive and enthusiasm, and she suddenly felt very fond of her quieter father and slipped her hand into his so that he shouldn't feel that all his children had deserted him.

As they came out of the studio Inigo's lights were on and the playground had turned back into a garden. The trees had haloes and threw mysterious shadows and the scene looked as though it was waiting for some romantic intrigue. Moth could see Miss Lambert still surrounded by people in the library and windows kept lighting up all over the house as though some wild chase was in progress.

'What a lovely house,' said Mrs. Graham, but before Moth could point out her classroom, her mother was forced to attend to Mrs. Blundell-Smith who wanted to congratulate her on having such a lovely daughter who'd been so clever to win the prize. Moth gave up and winked at Tom. She was amused to see that his father was a retiring little man who never seemed to get a word in.

When they finally got back to Great-Aunt Marion's flat they found that she had arranged one of her special feasts and bought a whole row of beer cans for Uncle Rex who was famous for his thirst. They all sat up late, talking first about the school and how well Libby and

Moth had done and then about the past and the war and life in Australia.

Lyn and Toby fell asleep and when at last everyone else was ready for bed there was a great sorting out of rooms. Uncle Rex said he could sleep on a clothes-line and would be quite happy on the settee, Mr. and Mrs. Graham had Libby's room, and all the children piled into Moth's. There was plenty of room for lilos and camp beds and sleeping bags and Moth felt an outsider as the only one in a proper bed.

Although it was so late, she was too excited and happy to sleep. She had passed her exam so Miss Lambert couldn't complain, she would be back next year and so would Libby. 'And next year,' thought Moth, 'I'll work even harder, I'll believe in myself more, and I'll win a prize. Yes,' she decided as she thought over the evening, 'next year I'll beat Libby.'

Author's Note

This book couldn't have been written without the help of the following people, whom I would like to thank: Miss Patricia Nicholson of Hodder & Stoughton, whose idea it was in the first place and without whose enthusiasm I should never have got started; Miss Nesta Brooking of the Brooking School of Ballet, who let me watch some of the classes at her school and gave up valuable time to talking to me and giving me ideas; Mr. Robert Aickman, who suggested Moth's name and whose artistic advice was inspiring; Mrs. M. I. Jack, the principal of the Arts Educational Schools, who kindly invited me to an end-of-term show; Miss Carol Venn of the Imperial Society of Teachers of Dancing, who put up with tiresome questions about dancing examinations; and Miss Katherine Sorley Walker, who answered my queries about Australian dancers.

I should like to stress that the school I have described is purely imaginary, and that there are few opportunities for full-time training at the age of 11. However it's important to make an early start at dancing classes, and if you want to try and don't know of a good school, you can get advice from:

Imperial Society of Teachers of Dancing, Euston Hall, Birkenhead Street, London WC1H 8BE.

The Royal Academy of Dancing, 48 Vicarage Crescent, London SW11 3LT.

You may like to know that Moth bought her ballet shoes and leotard at Frederick Freed Ltd, 94 St. Martins Lane, London WC2, and found her ballet posters at Dance Books Ltd, 9 Cecil Court, London WC2, a bookshop overflowing with dance books, magazines and photographs.

The theatres Moth and Libby bought came from Pollock's Toy Museum, 1 Scala Street, London W1. (Scala Street is between Tottenham Court Road and Charlotte Street – nearest Underground: Goodge Street.) You can buy the theatres in person or by post – Pollocks send them all over the world. The Museum is open every day except Sundays and Bank Holidays from 10 a.m. to 5 p.m.

If you want to see *La Fille mal gardée* – or any of the other ballets danced by the Royal Ballet or the Sadler's Wells Royal Ballet – you can get details of performances and dates by sending a stamped addressed envelope to the Marketing Department, Royal Opera House, Covent Garden, London WC2. Remember that both companies don't only dance in London, so ask if they're coming your way. It isn't easy to get tickets, especially for Covent Garden, so book well in advance or be prepared to queue on the day.

If you're really interested in ballet, you'll want to know more about it, so here are some books to keep a special look out for:

Balanchine's Festival of Ballet by George Balanchine, W. H. Allen, 1978.
A fat book that gives details of 404 ballets, with their stories and background information about the choreographers and dancers who created them. Balanchine himself is a famous choreographer, and there's a fascinating account of life in the Russian Ballet in the days before the Revolution. He also answers questions about ballet and gives advice about dancing as a career, from the American point of view. Although this is an expensive book, it's a ballet companion for life.

The Children of Theatre Street by Patricia Barnes, Phaidon, 1979.
The Imperial Ballet School in Theatre Street, St Petersburg, was the most famous ballet school in the world. All the names were changed after the Revolution, but the Vaganova Choreographic Institute, as it is now called, still produces outstanding dancers like Rudolf Nureyev, Natalia Makarova and Mikhail Baryshnikov. This book gives a short history of the school and tells you what it is like to be a pupil there today. It is based on a film (which has been shown in London) and there are many photographs taken from

the film showing the pupils at class and rehearsing for the graduation performance that decides their fate: which company they will be asked to join.

The Beaver Book of Ballet by Robina Beckles Wilson, Beaver, 1979.
An introduction to learning to dance, with details of life at a ballet school, steps and exercises.

The Young Ballet Dancer by Liliana Cosi, Ward Lock, 1978.
This is an attractive looking book with lots of pictures of young dancers at the Bolshoi doing their exercises. It will help you to tell a plié from a battement (if you're not a dancer), but the history and ballet stories are very sketchy.

Sibley and Dowell by Nicholas Dromgoole, with photographs by Leslie Spatt, Collins, 1976.
Although you can't see this famous partnership any more, the superb photographs capture the beauty and excitement of their dancing and the text gives a fascinating glimpse of dancers' lives and how their roles look from the other side of the footlights.

Margot Fonteyn, autobiography, W. H. Allen, 1975 – also available as a Star Book paperback, 1976.
The extraordinary life-story of a magical star.

A Dancer's World by Margot Fonteyn, W. H. Allen, 1978.
Advice about how to enjoy all kinds of dancing by

the greatest dancer of the Royal Ballet. Don't miss the chapter by her mother describing how Dame Margot first started dancing, and the answers to a lot of practical questions.

Better Ballet by Richard Glasstone, Kaye and Ward, 1977.
Mr Glasstone is a teacher at White Lodge, and the pupils there posed for the many photographs illustrating the steps and movements used in classical ballet.

Life at the Royal Ballet School by Camilla Jessel, Methuen, 1979.
Lots of photographs showing you what it's like to be a pupil at White Lodge, the junior section of the Royal Ballet School. It covers every stage from auditions through to the final year when the best pupils move on to the Upper School, and it begins with the warning words, 'This book is about the grinding hard work of training for ballet. . . . a study of a struggle – to get better – and better – and better.'

Ballet Stories by Joan Lawson, Ward Lock, 1978.
The stories of fourteen popular ballets told in simple terms and well illustrated in colour and black and white. Should help you decide which ballets you most want to see.

Enjoying Ballet by Jean Richardson, Beaver Books, 1977.
A handy paperback that tells you how a ballet is created, what makes a good dancer, and how dancers

are trained, and takes a look at the history of ballet and some of today's best known companies, productions and stars.

A Young Person's Guide to Ballet by Noel Streatfeild, Warne, 1975.
The story of two children aged nine who become interested in ballet and set out to find out all about it. Noel Streatfield also wrote *Ballet Shoes*, the famous story about the Fossil children, one of whom wanted desperately to become a dancer.

The Royal Ballet/Sadler's Wells Royal Ballet Yearbook.
If you've been to any of their productions recently, you might like this illustrated souvenir which has articles and lots of photographs. On sale at the Royal Opera House or can be bought by post.

THE END

ELIZABETH GOUDGE

SMOKY-HOUSE

Five children lived in Smoky-House at Faraway, with their two dogs, Spot and Sausage, and Matilda the donkey. Sometimes on a moonlit night they could see a ship lying at anchor off the coast. They knew then that there were smugglers about; but even the fear of the Man-with-the-Red-Handkerchief did little to disturb the peace of the village. The REAL danger began the evening the Fiddler stepped out of the sunset; and then it was up to the children and the animals to save the people of Faraway.

KNIGHT BOOKS

JEAN WEBSTER

DADDY-LONG-LEGS

The story of Judy and her mysterious guardian is one of the most popular romances ever written, and it has been both filmed and made into a highly successful musical.

Judy, at seventeen is taken from an Institution, where she is the oldest orphan, and sent to college – at the expense of an amused and anonymous Trustee. A wavering, elongated shadow, once seen, is her only clue, and this induces her to call him Daddy-Long-Legs.

KNIGHT BOOKS

THE BLACK STALLION

WALTER FARLEY

Alec Ramsay was on the long voyage home from India, where his uncle had taught him the one thing in the world he had always wanted to do – ride a horse. But now that was over, how could a boy living in New York City ever hope to have a horse of his own?

Alec first saw the Black Stallion when his ship docked at a small Arabian port on the Red Sea. Little did he know then that this magnificent wild horse was destined to play a very important part in his young life and that the strange understanding which grew between them would lead them through untold dangers to adventure in America.

KNIGHT BOOKS